SURRENDERED II

BY

PEGGY PATRICK

ENDORSEMENTS

I love to hear stories about how God meets our needs. Sometimes it is in the most unexpected ways. In this story Laura has had a difficult life. She thinks she knows what she needs and proceeds to take care of it on her own. It only causes her more pain. God knows what we need and we need to wait on Him. Laura learns this lesson in a dramatic way that the reader will never forget. Laura's life will never be the same after her encounter with God. Excellent work.
*****jamasc

It's so nice to read a Christian-based story with characters who have real-life problems, but whose story makes you cry and laugh with them. I loved the first book and couldn't wait for the second to come out. It was worth the wait. Keep writing and telling great, Christian-based stories.
*****Pam

I read the first novel that Mrs. Patrick wrote and I really enjoyed the book very much. But the Surrendered 2 was even better. It was like I was watching a movie as I was reading both books. I laughed and I did, I'll admit, for a 59 year old man, Yes I shed some tears too. Keep writing because you have a real talent for writing. The miracle with the colt was awesome and inspiring to say the least.
*****Buddy W. Lake

Loved this book... It's a book that is hard to put down.. couldn't wait to see what was going to happen next.
*****Dorothy

I read Mrs. Patricks first book and could not wait for her second one to come out. It was all I expected it to be. A very Christian book with morals. Did not want to put it down. Great story line, good humor and wholesome. Can't wait till her next book come's out she is a a very creatative lady.
*****Beth

DEDICATION

This book is dedicated to the Lord Jesus Christ who has, so mercifully and patiently taught me how wide, how long, how high and how deep is His love toward us all...even to the fullness of performing His most extravagant miracles.

AUTHOR'S NOTE

As I wrote Surrendered II, I was awakened suddenly early one morning. Instantly, an incident was brought to my mind that happened several years ago. I personally witnessed this event and as I was reminded of it, I saw it replayed in my inner vision, but instead of the actual people that were involved, I *saw* the event played out by the characters in Surrendered II. I knew the Lord was instructing me to write that event into this novel.

I wrote the story as fully detailed as it actually happened...the amazing account of how God chose to instantly...supernatually heal a dying horse to prove His existence to a professed atheist and then her subsequent profession of faith in the Lord Jesus Christ.

With the exception of that event told within this novel, Surrendered II is purely a work of fiction. I sincerely hope you will enjoy reading this book as much as I enjoyed writing it. I welcome your comments and may be contacted at peggynpat@yahoo.com.

ACKNOWLEDGEMENTS

Thank you to my brilliant daughter, Lisa Sandmann, for your hard work and perserverance in all phases of this book. I love you. I owe you!

Thank you to my husband, Pat, for keeping my coffee cup full for months.

Thank you to a very special lady in my life, Mama Mae Wiggins, my greatest encourager.

CHAPTER ONE

"Laura Parker, you have lost your ever-loving mind!" She whispered those words to her reflection in the full length mirror on the wall of the western wear store. Then she turned and sashayed airily across the floor, ignoring the fact that her legs felt like stilts. Just the toes of her new taupe roper boots stuck out under the equally new boot cut Wrangler jeans. The *pre-washed* tag in the waist band pricked her back with every gyrating move she made, needling her to call the whole thing off.

She would have promptly obeyed, but Andy was just too excited about it. His little eyes were beaming, set back under a brand new wide-brimmed straw hat. Laura smiled at how handsome he looked. Her son had endured a lot for his five years of life and if spending a week playing cowboy in the wilds of Wyoming could restore a little innocuous energy to his wounded spirit, it would be worth every minute.

By the time she changed back into her flip flops and beige Capri's, the salesgirl had her new cowgirl duds sacked up. She paid the pricey amount for the *cowboy* clothes for her and Andy, then headed the few blocks down the street to her vehicle.

Outside the morning Texas sun was warming rapidly. More than once, Laura caught a glimpse of a passerby smiling down at Andy and his new *dude* outfit. His unscuffed rough-out leather boots clicked proudly.

"Mom?" Andy raised his face upward, squinting against the sunlight and she looked down, surprised at his serious tone. "Do you think Dad would like me to be a cowboy?"

A surge of emotion welled in her and she looked away in case he might misinterpret the sudden strain on her face. She wasn't quite eighteen when she had married Matthew Parker. Having been raised in extreme poverty, Matt had become her light at the end of the tunnel. They met the day her mother died, and he had been by her side from that day on. Marrying him had ended her poverty stricken way of life, moving her up to a modest home with all the trimmings of middle class America.

He would be elated with this upcoming trip. But then, if he was here, this trip would not be happening. That thought turned bittersweet as her mind recalled her total obstinacy to her husband's mention of selling their home and throwing in with his boyhood friend, J.D., as a partner in some sort of ranching operation. According to Matt, the two had planned this during their teen years after spending many weekends together playing cowboy on a neighboring ranch. Matt had spoken often of the old bachelor cowboy he called Mr. Lex who had taught him and his friend, J.D. how to rope and ride and string barb wire.

And some fifteen or so years later, according to Matt, J.D. had shown up unannounced at their door, passing through town with a head full of boyhood dreams to share with her husband.

Laura had been out on a rare shopping event that day. Rare because Matthew never allowed her out alone, let alone with money to spend. Laura remembered his insistence that she and Andy go for the day. She remembered that day so well because it only happened that once.

When Matt told her that evening about JDs visit and offer for them to partner on this ranch venture up north, she didn't try to hear him out about the plan. It was the only time she could remember ever speaking up for herself. Ever daring to. The suggestion was so outrageous, she had shut her ears to any serious talk about it. She feared returning to the meager way of living she'd been raised in—never enough food, rags for clothes, and bug infested housing. Not to mention her notion that country life was all those things and worse. She had held her ground until the subject was abandoned.

Remembering was painful, and she fought with a rising tide of guilt the idea that she should plan a trip of that nature now. Matt was killed in a car wreck almost a year ago. Even though she was still trying to sort through her grief and settle fully into the swing of being a single parent, she believed Matt would have enjoyed the idea of her decision to take Andy on this vacation. More than anything, Andy needed a fresh breath of happy excitement.

She smiled down at her son. "Yes, Andy...your dad would be *way* proud of you."

He grinned broadly beneath his curved hat brim.

By the time she packed four traveling bags, it was almost 10pm. She scanned her list of things to do and checked off everything she'd written down. Canceled the mail, stopped the newspaper and cleaned out perishables from the refrigerator. Lastly, her late model Escalade SUV had been serviced.

With nothing left to do except load up in the morning and go, she was just realizing that she had never undertaken the feat of making a trip alone. Matt had always taken care of every detail—taken such good care of *her*. Now, here she was, ready to drive off to another part of the country with no one but herself to depend on.

She picked up the brochure from the desk in the study and read the High Point Dude Ranch activity section again. It certainly wasn't appealing to her city girl blood. This ranch was in Wyoming, near Jackson. Horses to ride. *Ugh*. A hay ride along a rushing stream and chuck wagon *grub* for every meal. The pamphlet to this place was mixed in with some of Matt's papers in the desk.

More than anything, she was thankful that Matthew had left her without financial worries. A home insurance policy had paid the balance of the note off and his life insurance had provided plenty of cushion for a few years.

Andy was asleep and she decided she had better do the same. She had a long drive ahead of her. After slipping into pink silk pajama leggings and an oversized white V-neck T-shirt, she turned a circle in front of the floor length mirror on the back of the bedroom door. Weight had never been an issue for her, but tonight she noticed she must have dropped some by the way her clothes were hanging off of her shoulders and hips. The girl in the western store made her laugh when she remarked that Laura was so thin in her new jeans, she could hula hoop a cheerio. She giggled at the remembrance.

She fished a hair pick out of her purse where it lay on the foot of her bed and ran it through her bouncy medium length layers. Her multi-shades of blonde were natural and always commanded compliments from women wanting to duplicate the color. It seemed odd that others noticed her in ways that she never paid attention to. She was simply Laura Parker—Andy's mom. With that, she turned out her light and slept soundly.

By four the next morning, Laura glanced in her rear view mirror at the single front porch light that she'd left burning. Andy bedded down in the back seat, his full head of sandy blonde hair sinking deeply into a fluffy pillow as she aimed the pearl white Cadillac north toward what she hoped would be a great adventure for her son. For his sake, she would buck up and take it like a cowgirl. The thought created an image in her mind's eye that made her laugh.

She had considered flying instead of attempting a two day long haul behind the wheel alone with Andy. But the trip proved uneventful and she felt proud of herself and totally exhausted when she finally pulled up in front of the big gray frame ranch house. Andy was already working on another night's sleep.

After stepping out of the car, Laura stretched her legs. Her eyes focused on *Headquarters* that swung on what looked like a long, flat slab of driftwood above the steps to the porch, where a floodlight yellowed the front of the house. Before she could move a step, the screen door of the house opened suddenly, then slapped shut behind a young man who came quickly down the steps skipping every other one.

"Mrs. Parker, we've been waiting for you...No trouble, I hope?" His friendliness pacified the trepidation she had fought off and on for two days.

"No, just lots of miles."

She simulated a smile through her exhaustion, absently raking a hand through her hair and trying to take in the dim-lighted appearance of this rancher. He was tall and lanky with a black cowboy hat pushed back on his head revealing the face of a twenty year old. His faded jeans looked as though they had put in a rough day. He bent down to peer into her car window.

"Andy's asleep in the back seat," she answered his silent question.

He straightened up and took a close, but impersonal scan of her as he thrust out his hand. "Pleasure to meet you, Mrs. Parker. Donny Brandon."

"I'm just Laura," she offered and shook hands. She felt comfortable with this young man. The twinkles in his eyes that lit the darkness between them spoke of friendly and kind.

"Ok, just Laura." His smile was large. "I'm guessing you could use about forty winks yourself. Hop in and I'll park you two across the drive there at your cabin." He stood beside the driver's door and waited for her to walk around to the other side and get in, then slid behind the wheel.

In seconds the young cowboy pulled in alongside a very small log cabin nestled beneath a cluster of huge pine trees. Laura carried suitcases while he deposited a sleepy Andy under warm blankets in a small bedroom just his size.

"Phone number to headquarters is on the wall in the kitchen. Don't hesitate to call it...Night," he said over his shoulder as he closed the door behind himself.

Okay. Now what? She took a quick survey of the small, but cozy atmosphere of the cabin. A little kitchenette was tucked back in the corner of the room with a short bar separating it from the living area. A rock fireplace topped with a split log mantel resembled one she'd seen in one of Andy's storybooks. It almost seemed animated. Very cozy. She recognized the fake logs stacked haphazardly inside the firebox. Yes, *gas logs!* She walked over and turned the knob located close to the floor and presto...a bluish yellow flame shot up giving the room a warm golden glow. Matt had installed a smaller electric version in their bedroom, but this just seemed to set a homey atmosphere in this little rustic log hut. She felt hugged.

Laura shook her head and laughed at her ridiculous surmising, as she turned down the flame to a tiny flicker. She was just delirious from the long drive and total exhaustion. The bathroom was small enough to stand in one spot and do just about everything without taking more than one step in any direction. She showered because there was no tub and fell into the wall to wall queen size bed. At least she had a room to herself. Tomorrow she would take a more thorough tour.

A loud banging suddenly aroused her from a deep sleep. It took her a few seconds to remember where she was. Lifting herself up by one hand, she focused her eyes on the flaming streaks of sunrise out her window, then fell back onto her pillow. She pushed her tousled locks away from her face and stretched until her body begged for release. The banging came again, this time intermingled with a familiar voice.

"Mrs. Parker?"

She jumped up and fumbled in a suitcase for her terry robe, tied the sash and swung open the door to the familiar voice.

"It's Laura and good morning."

"Laura...Laura," he repeated with a grin. "Mornin...Hope you got some good sleep." He walked in and placed a plate of piping hot breakfast on the kitchen bar. "Thought you'd be about ready for this. The rest of the guests have left for a morning trail ride. I didn't want your victuals to get wasted."

Laura blinked sleepy eyes at the single serving of egg, sausage and buttered biscuit, then glanced at the Mr. Coffee on the counter. "I'm not much on breakfast. Takes a couple cups of coffee to get me percolating first...pun intended," she chuckled. "But Andy will take care of that as soon as he wakes up." At his blank look, she added quickly, "It was sweet of you to bring it over...We sort of blew our first morning."

-336   "No, not at all. I'm just surprised you didn't know about the boy. He showed up for breakfast with the rest of us and rode out with my brother, Jesse, on the trail ride."

"What?" She was wide awake now. "He's never been on a horse. I mean...he's never..."

"Relax." Donny put up a hand to stop her panic. "He's ridin' double with Jesse...Nothin' to worry about." He grinned and shook his head. "That's quite an eager little guy you've got."

His easy manner relaxed her fear.

As he turned to leave, he shot over his shoulder, "Soon as you're dressed and fed up...come out to the barn there across the drive. I'll show you around the place."

"I'll do that. Thanks."

He tipped his hat and strode out.

She felt her face blush slightly, figuring she sounded as rattled as she looked. The feeling worsened as she caught his one-sided sort of smile, partly shadowed by the brim of his hat. He was a handsome kid in his denim chambray long sleeves and skinny long legged jeans. But then she had read somewhere that all cowboys were supposed to be good looking.

After getting the coffee started, she quickly showered, then dressed in jeans, boots and a soft pink T-shirt. A white scarf tied her hair back. She was glad she had purchased the boots. They just seemed to fit in with the atmosphere. *A real dude,* she thought, but she was comfortable enough.

Lingering an extra minute in front of the bathroom mirror, she sucked in a deep breath, prematurely deciding this vacation might turn out better than she'd first thought. It was just a gut feeling. She couldn't really put her finger on why the subtle change in her attitude about how her next two weeks would be spent. She hadn't been successful at drumming up interest in this trip, other than for Andy's enjoyment, but suddenly she was finding herself looking forward to what lay beyond her cabin door.

Maybe it had actually begun yesterday with the accomplishment of the drive here. There was a new sense of freedom, and an awareness of her surroundings of herself and of the fact that she was just realizing how sheltered her life had been. Funny, she had never known she was so closed off from life until she had taken on planning and driving this trip. It was like peeking out over the edge of a box after discovering there was no lid on it.

The plate of breakfast was stone cold, but just as well, since her appetite was not awakened yet.

Minutes later, after downing a large mug of hot coffee, she was ready to discover just exactly what the dudes around here do.

By the time she stepped outside, she felt more refreshed than she had been in a long time, discovering it was one of those fine bright days that springtime brings, clear and crystal-like with the sun squinting down on the past night's dew. The air was crisp and breezing slightly through the tall pine trees that scented the air. A deep breath invigorated her senses and lightened her steps toward the big paint peeled red barn.

The barn doors were open. She stood inside and waited until her eyes grew accustomed to the darkness. It smelled of animals. Horses, she guessed. Soon she could see a long wide alley running through the structure with stalls lining the full length of it on either side. Some were empty, others occupied, inquisitive heads hanging over the latched gates. Ears were perked up, eyes staring at her. One solid black horse, its mane long and silky, caught her attention. The beauty of the animal tempted her over for a touch.

"That's nice...nice pony." She eased her hand to his nose, then braved stroking the flowing mane.

"I could have guessed you'd have an eye for beauty." The voice startled her even though she knew it was Donny. She jerked her hand away and turned around.

"I didn't hear you walk up."

"That's the Indian blood in me," he grinned. "Go ahead...pet him. More attention he gets...better he likes it." Donny pushed his hat back on his head as though to give it a rest, bringing his smoky eyes out into the open. His thumbs rested just inside his belt buckle as he stood staring down at her, grinning. This kid couldn't get much better looking without causing a female stampede, she decided.

"When are the trail riders due back?" she asked and glanced at her watch. It was nine o'clock. "They've been gone for hours already."

"Almost another hour before they get in. How about I show you the rest of the place? Take about that long to see it all."

"Sure...I'd love it." She decided to relax and settle in. She was here for two weeks—of fun.

"Let's just start right here." He reached both arms over the gate and roughly rubbed the horse's neck. "Laura, meet Rebel Man. He's the real man of this outfit. He belongs to Jesse. For a stallion he's gentle...but Jesse is picky about his handling. Loves this old horse more than he likes to eat," he said with a grin.

She was beginning to wonder about Jesse Brandon. His telephone voice was deep and he'd been very much to the point in making her reservations. Almost rude. She hoped he was as responsible as Donny said in taking care of Andy. She dragged her attention back to her guide as he expounded some facts about other horses behind the stall gates.

"That chestnut mare there is due to foal. Might be a little trouble...so we're keeping an eye on her."

Soon they were crossing the yard which was bordered on three sides by long stretches of log fences. More fences seemed to cross each other, separating several small pasture areas. The land was rolling and grassy, except for the distance mountain peaks that guarded the fertile valley harboring High Point Ranch. Truly beautiful. Mares and new colts grazed and galloped in the spring sun in the front pasture. Others seemed to laze in the early morning warm rays.

The pair trailed across the front yard of the big ranch house, pausing only briefly as Donny explained that he and Jesse called it home while it served as a second home for a little woman he called Martha, who cleaned up after the two sloppy bachelors.

She caught the fact that neither of these brothers were married. Maybe she hadn't been entirely wrong about this kind of lifestyle. There didn't seem to be any women that lived here.

She followed Donny's lead around to the opposite side of the house, surprised at the sudden change in the scenery. A large painted concrete slab spread across the back yard was complete with a band stage. Tables and chairs decorated a circle outside on the green lawn. Colorful flags were hung in streamers from inside of the pavilion roof that covered the concrete floor and across the yard above the seating area.

Donny noticed her pleasure at the sight. "Every woman loves a party and I can see you're no exception. Like to dance, Laura?"

"It's been a while since I've been on a dance floor...but yes, I love it." In truth, Matt had taken her dancing once.

"Good. We do a lot of it around here. At least a couple parties a week." He took off his hat and swung it around in front of himself, bowing like a gentleman. "And you are looking at the number one two-stepper in all of Wyoming."

Laura laughed at his conceited humor, deciding a little of that conceit was probably genuine. But she couldn't help but like him. She noticed that his bareheaded features produced an even younger image.

A ruckus erupted on the opposite side of the pavilion, turning both of their heads toward it. Laura shaded her eyes from the sun's glare, catching sight of an aging old-timer, a covered wagon and a mule. The man was waving a black cooking pot toward the creature who was not disturbed in the least.

"Git! Go on now." A gentle bop on the nose with the pan went unheeded by the hoofed intruder. "I'll have your big ears pinned to the barn wall next time I ketch you in my sugar bowl...Now, git!" A harder wallop sent the mule in the opposite direction, leaving the old man mumbling under his breath.

Laura's guide doubled over, spurring her own amusement. Regaining his composure, Donny casually put an arm around Laura's shoulder and guided her in the direction of the wagon.

"Come and meet my favorite partner," he told her, still chuckling.

Seeing the pair approaching, the old man quickly yanked off his sloppy hat and stuck it under his arm. He wiped his hands on his soiled apron.

"Cook, I want you to meet our newest and prettiest guest at High Point, Laura Parker."

"Howdy, Miz Parker." They exchanged a quick handshake.

"Cook here feeds this bunch three times a day out of this chuck wagon." Donny licked his lips. "And he can cook ever bit as good as I can dance." His laughter erupted again. "What's all the racket? Aint you giving old Sally enough attention anymore?"

"That durn mule." He glanced at Laura, a slight grin pulling his whiskered face. That four-legged critter ain't worth making bear bait out of. Why I oughta..."

"You oughta just pipe down and get a fire under that stew... 'cause if anything ever happened to that mule...I'd have you to bury and you know it. Those tired, hungry riders may do it anyway if their lunch isn't hot when they get here."

The old man shook his head, still grinning and waved the pair off so he could tend to business.

Donny and Laura walked back toward the barn, talking casually about the usual schedule at the ranch. Donny had taken on a more serious composure. "The breakfast bell rings by six, for lunch around eleven and for supper by five-thirty. When you hear it...just come running. That boy of yours can show you the ropes about that."

He glanced at his watch, then Laura followed his gaze across the pasture. A string of approximately six or seven horses carrying worn riders was making its way toward them. She squinted at the big man on the lead horse, deciding that must be Jesse, but anxiously waited for some sign of Andy. Finally she sighed in relief as his little cotton-top head peered around from behind the man.

"Hi, Mom!" He waved wildly grinning from ear to ear.

Without looking behind him, the cowboy grasped Andy's arm and swung him down from the huge animal, setting him easily on his feet, never so much as glancing at Laura. The sullen indifference on his face caused her to wonder if Andy had made a pest of himself all morning.

The saddle made a creaking noise as she observed the man dismounting. He was well over six foot tall and built like a tackle for the Dallas Cowboys. A giant of a man. She found it impossible to move her eyes away from him.

His broad chest and shoulders were covered with a leather buckskin jacket. Long threads of leather dangled from the full length of the sleeves and made a v-shape across his wide chest. Coal black silky hair lay just below his collar and protruded around his face under an off-white cowboy hat. His eyes were shaded by his hat brim, but his strong jaw was lined with sideburns that extended down his face and formed a full-faced short growth of beard. His full mustache was neatly trimmed. She watched as he slid the jacket off and hung it on his saddle. The white long-sleeved western shirt, tucked into dark denim jeans seemed to accentuate his solid lean muscled form and gave him a whole new look of sophistication and class that was hidden underneath the coat.

Small fingers wiggled their way into her hand and brought her back to herself. Embarrassment heated her face, realizing she had been staring, probably with her mouth open. But no one seemed to have noticed. She squeezed Andy's hand and peered into his shining eyes. His excitement was running in high gear. She knew she would have to reprimand him for running off without her knowledge, but decided to do so privately. She could hardly undermine his happiness. It had been so long since she'd seen his face spread with that much joy.

"Looks like you got broke in right, partner." Donny said. He walked over to tussle Andy's hair, then summoned his brother over to join them. Laura watched the big man approach, taking long, slow strides, stopping an arm's length from her.

"Jesse, meet Laura Parker. She's had the grand tour of the grounds. I'd say she's ready for the big time."

"Ma'am." Jesse tipped his hat and stood straight and stiff, acting every bit as rude as he'd sounded on the phone when Laura had called for reservations.

She hoped she read the taut lines of his jaw right, that he was tired from his ride and not angry as it appeared. His low pitched drawl was gruff, matching the mountain man coat he had just taken off. She tilted her head back slightly, moving her eyes upward. "It's nice to meet you, Jesse." She swallowed, not sure that it was.

She felt herself cringe inwardly as his eyes made a scan of her from head to toe. His gaze roamed her face, finally stopping to fix a strange enigmatic frown into her own shocked stare. A slight quickening of her pulse caused her small fists to clench. Unable to break his silent perplexing contemplation of her, she expelled a slight sigh when his gaze fell downward and just to her side.

A hint of a smile faintly pulled at the corners of his mouth as he stepped just past her and took Andy's shoulder and prodded him playfully ahead in the direction of the chuck wagon. "How's your appetite, son?" he asked.

"It's wild and woolly," Andy answered as he spread a wide grin up at his big friend. Jesse threw his head back and laughed as Andy deliberately stretched his short legs trying to keep in step with him.

Laura turned her head and watched them walk away. "Wild and woolly?" she repeated to herself. Where on earth had he picked up that language? Other weary riders began trailing behind them and blocked her view of the pair.

She fought a surge of anger rising until it turned into dejection. Jesse's hostility was shocking and disturbed her even more now since he obviously was not trying to get rid of a pesky kid. She felt attacked, but reminded herself that this trip was for Andy, and that part seemed to be working real well.

Donny gave no indication that he'd noticed as he circled his arm around her waist and forced her toward the crowd where Cook was sounding the big bell. "If we don't get in line...we're going to be two might hungry dudes when that bell rings again."

She laughed, suddenly bored with her dramatics about Jesse.

The low murmur of voices mingled with groans of saddle pains as some of the guests settled themselves around the table and in chairs spread around the outside of the pavilion. Others sprawled out on the cool dry grass. A fragrance of honeysuckle tinged the air while a steaming pot of stew was sending up smoke signals behind the chuck wagon.

Laura consciously stepped just out of Donny's touch before approaching the throng of people. She noticed an older gentleman nodding in her direction, then another looking her way from another table. She knew they were misreading her and Donny. So what if they were. She smiled back.

Lunch was enjoyable and she was glad when Andy appeared to plop down on the grass between them.

"Hi there." She put her arm around Andy's shoulders and squeezed. "Aren't you about to wind down yet, kiddo?"

"Heck no, Mom. Jesse said we get to ride on a hay wagon tonight and I get to help him drive the horses...but I have to ask you first. Can I, Mom?"

"Wait a minute...Slow down." Laura couldn't help but laugh at his excitement. How glad she was that she had brought him here. But she knew she couldn't allow him to monopolize this rancher's time. He did have a lot of other guests. "I'll talk to Mr. Brandon, Andy, to be sure it's okay."

"But he asked me to help him...I know it's all right. He's gone now, but he'll be back later on." Andy stood and bounced from one foot to the other, still beside himself with excitement.

"Tell the boy he can go before he pops his buttons off. And don't worry about him bothering my brother. I've never known him to take on a sidekick unless he wanted to." Donny spoke up in Andy's defense.

"Oh boy!" Andy shouted and jumped up and down, then disappeared before his mother had time to protest.

Nevertheless, she made up her mind to check it out with Jesse.

Peggy Patrick

***

CHAPTER TWO

Before six-thirty that evening, Laura managed a much needed nap for herself. Donny had taken Andy on for the afternoon, and after the rush of activities, including a hiking tour, her muscles demanded relief.

She glanced at the Timex around her wrist. She had fifteen minutes to make the hay ride and her silently made appointment with the ranch boss had to be kept before that.

The sudden twist in the pit of her stomach annoyed her. She wasn't frightened of the man, but there was something different about him. Maybe his contrast in appearance to the other men here—or to anyone she'd ever met before, but her impression of him today certainly left something to be desired. His manner was reckless and rude. But, she decided that was his choice.

A quick brush through her hair and a little pink lipstick and blusher on her cheeks made her at least *look* awake.

Another glance at her watch said she was five minutes late. Racing outside, she found a long wide flatbed wagon full of oblong hay bales and people. Four horses were harnessed in some weird looking contraption waiting patiently.

"Hey, Laura...Come on and hop up!" Donny yelled across the yard and slapped the hay seat beside him on the wagon.

She made her way toward the wagon and strained her neck around until she could see Andy perched on the driver's seat beside Jesse. She changed direction and headed toward the front of the wagon. Just before she reached within hearing distance, she glanced up to see the big cowboy staring at her. He had turned his head to purposefully look at her and she knew full well he was aware that she was coming to say something to him.

Something in his look was hard and unapproachable. She felt her throat tighten until it blocked any sound she might have forced out. He looked away and as if to cut her off, his graveled voice shouted, "All aboard! Here we go!"

Frozen in her tracks, Laura fought a drowning surge of anger at his arrogance. It was *not* her imagination. His uncivil attitude was definitely directed at her.

It was Donny who forced her stiffened muscles to relax when he appeared beside her, gently taking her hand and steering her to the wagon. She felt his hands on either side of her waist, easily lifting her weight. One short jump and he was perched beside her.

Despite the circumstances, Laura became engulfed with the unusual beauty of her surroundings. The winding road was rough and bumpy, but she enjoyed her view of the gorgeous grass-floored valley that wound in dips and curves through the hillside. The Snake River curved in and out through the middle of the valley, the deep blue water highlighted with soft streaks of orange from the now setting sun.

She listened with an eager fascination as Donny explained the difference in trees—fir, pine, spruce and other evergreens were this area's claim to mountain forests. "Big game animals are my passion," he explained. "Deer roam the desert floor as well as the mountains. Keep your eyes peeled...you might glimpse a bear or moose. Mountain goats and sheep live in these parts...And elk for sure."
-336 He raised his voice, almost shouting. "Anybody here like to catch big fish?" the crowd responded with a few 'yeas' and an uneven round of applause. "All right," he answered. "You're my kind of people. You'll get your chance to wrestle with a fat trout."

Laura allowed her attention to wander to the driver and his little helper. They seemed to be totally engrossed in conversation, but she couldn't hear them. They were probably discussing birds and trout, neither of which she was particularly intrigued with.

The hay ride was enjoyable, but apprehension knotted her stomach when the wagon rolled into the ranch yard and pulled to a halt. She knew it was because of the unfinished business that Jesse had silently begun with her.

After helping her off her perch, Donny swung Andy upon his shoulders, then stalked over to where a couple of ranch hands were unhitching the team.

Laura saw Jesse stride off alone toward the barn and decided it was time. She felt disgusted at her rubbery legs and flipped over stomach, but headstrong determination kept her moving.

She had to literally force her hand to the wood handle and pull it open. The place appeared empty except for Rebel Man's excited pacing in his narrow stall. She glanced around for some sight of Jesse, without success, then walked slowly toward the animal, not knowing what else to do at that moment.

"What is it, fella?" she whispered over the stall gate. "Bet you'd like to get out of here and run those fancy legs off... wouldn't you?"

Although there was no sound, she instinctively knew someone was behind her. Turning, she found herself staring into Jesse's black matted hairy chest where his shirt was hanging unbuttoned and pulled out of his jeans. Slowly she raised her eyes to find, *was it contempt,* glaring down at her? She stood still, her face blank from shock. One urge said turn and run while another told her to serve him a large slice of her irritated mind. Before she could respond, he spoke first.

"What can I do for you, Mrs. Parker?" His tone was low and gravelly, lips barely moving.

With great effort, she willed herself calm before she spoke. "I wanted to talk to you about Andy."

His eyebrows rose slightly to urge her on.

"I...I was afraid he might be working on wearing out his welcome." She hated the quiver in her voice.

"Quite the opposite, Mrs. Parker. As a matter of fact...I thoroughly believe in young children being given a lot of attention. When it comes from the right place...a kid doesn't feel a need to seek it from strangers." His voice was level and calm. She felt her entire body stand up straight, defiance moving right up to her eyebrows. Had he slapped her, her eyes couldn't spread any wider. "How dare you." Her voice came in a controlled whisper. "How dare you attack my...my... motherhood."

She swallowed hard to pull back some control for herself. "He...Andy has had a terrible tragedy to adjust to the past months."

His steely gaze narrowed on her, then she felt, rather than saw, his towering frame relax.

"Maybe if his mother could adjust to it...he'd stand a better chance. He's a smart kid and kids can spot deception without looking for it."

She fought to swallow the lump in her throat. Losing out, she turned and walked quickly out of the barn. She ran across the lane into the privacy of her cabin.

Jesse's words were cruel, but she wondered, even more now, about Andy's conversation with him on the hay ride that evening. She couldn't demand to know what he had said. He was entitled to his thoughts. At least he was expressing them to someone, if not her.

She tried to conceal the lingering traces of tears when Andy rushed in a while later and forced herself to laugh with him in his excitement of the day. She relaxed only after he was tucked into bed and asleep.

After a hot shower, she slipped into her pink silk lounging pants and long roomy T-shirt and draped herself across the length of the love seat in front of the fireplace. A tiny flicker licked through the gas logs to knock the evening chill from the cabin. She wished for once she could wiggle her nose like Samantha on the old television series, Bewitched, and presto, time with its magic healing power would move ahead instantly and relieve her stricken spirit.

She brushed a fresh overflow of tears from her cheeks. She had never been a cry baby, but had learned very early in life that that didn't help anything. Now she couldn't seem to shut it off. Grief was a strange thing. Matt had been her rock for so long. He took care of her and Andy's needs night and day. He was always there. Now, he wasn't. Emotionally she had been what someone had called, shell-shocked. She knew at some point there would be some terrible trauma, a time of anger, of desperately wanting to turn back the time to the way life was before Matt's accident. But that never came for her. Maybe that's what was happening now.

Footsteps sounded outside the door, and she was glad for the interruption of this ridiculous blubbering. She knew it was Donny coming to check on her and Andy. She waited for the knock, forced a smile on her face, then opened the door.

She almost choked at the sight of Jesse towering in front of her. "More deception?" he quipped, noticing her fixed smile.

Without thinking, her hand tightened on the door frame, then she slammed it toward him. He blocked its force with his palm, holding it open.

"Be careful who you're slamming doors on, young woman." He stepped inside and pushed the door shut behind him. His glance went past her, then back. "Is the boy asleep?" His voice was low, his eyes gentle enough.

She nodded, unable to summon her voice. A man who would brazenly force his way into her cabin was capable of forcing himself on her as well, but she wasn't afraid of him. Just royally ticked. She stood still waiting for him to make the first move.

Finally, "You came looking for me tonight with something on your mind...I don't believe you said what it was. You've got some unfinished business with me. I'm here to see that it gets finished."

She was thinking one of them had lost their mind and she was sure it wasn't her. "I have no idea what you're talking about, Mr. Brandon."

He waved his hand loosely toward the little couch. "Sit down. We've got some talking to do."

"I'm reasonably sure we have nothing more to say to each other and I would like you to leave...if you don't mind."

"I do mind. I mind a lot of things that's been going on around here since you arrived and we're going to fix a couple of them right now. Sit down."

When she didn't move, he took hold of her upper arm and moved her gradually backward until she stumbled against the edge of the love seat, then urged her to a sitting position before releasing her. He held his weight with one hand on the back of the seat, then leaned over her with his face a whisper away from hers. His voice was solid gravel.

"First off, if you think a stay at a big dude ranch up north is the place to hunt you a man...well...you could be right. But for you, lady...Donny's not it! He's an eighteen year old kid."

Laura's mouth dropped open, her eyes almost matching it's size. Was there no end to this jackass? As her shock subsided, a ripping anger besieged her as she tried to push him out of her face. He moved his head back just enough distance for her to bring up one hand and connect it with his cheek. She watched the flaming print of her hand burn into a whelp on his face before she felt herself being pulled to her feet. His free hand closed securely on her jaw as his mouth came down to return the slap in the form of a punishing kiss.

She struggled violently, but to no avail. She could do no more than allow the humiliation. He dropped her arm and brought his up around her back, arching her body in a steel-trap hold against his chest, body heat burning like a lighted furnace through her lounge clothes.

She had no idea when it happened, when he was no longer gripping her, holding her against him. His arms were around her, relaxed, and she was kissing him back.

Horrified at what she had just done, she pushed him back from her, easily escaping his unrestrained hold. The look on his face told her he was equally as surprised at the turn this meeting had taken. A wave of guilt washed over her then, thankfully suffocating the arousal that had come out of nowhere. He was looking at her like she had just landed a space ship.

"You're an animal," she spat at him, angrier with herself at the moment than him.

He spoke after several seconds. "Evidently the animal type appeals to you." His grin brought a flood of heat to her face. "And now that you know the type you prefer...you can keep your sights off my kid brother."

Angry tears trickled down. "That's a cruel thing to say. Donny was just being helpful. I know very well that he's just a kid...and I'm not here looking for..."

Her knees felt suddenly like they might buckle. Her strength ebbed away and she sat back down and covered her face with one hand. "This has turned out to be a big ugly mistake." Her eyes brimmed with fresh tears, spilling over to wet her face and hand. .

She caught the orange flicker of his cigarette lighter from the corner of her eye, her first indication that he had sat down beside her. He changed his mind and put the unlit cigarette in the ash tray on the lamp table beside him. His mood was quietly solaced.

"Andy talked to me about his father."

"So I assumed. Matt's death was hard on him," she stated flatly. She felt his eyes studying her intently.

"Kids seem to have a unique way of adjusting to circumstances and he's done a good job in my opinion. Don't you think it's time you tried some of the same?"

She turned then to look at him. Lord, what had Andy said to this man? His eyes were searching hers as though hunting for something in particular.

-336   "I don't know what you mean."

"Yes, you do. You know what love is about and the way you kissed me just now was not in response to *my* need."

The muscles in her stomach knotted up. She had allowed this stranger to uncover a vulnerability in her that she didn't know how to handle with it out in the open. He had forced it from her. She was a single woman and he was taking advantage of it.

The solution was obvious. Slowly and calmly she stood up and moved away from the couch a few steps, then turned to look into his questioning face.

"I want you to leave now, Andy...and I will do the same in the morning."

She spoke without emotion, but her heart jerked stupidly when she saw him stand up and come toward her, then stop a step away from touching her. His eyes held hers for a few agonizing seconds. She couldn't define what she saw in his face.

Finally he said, "When you're ready to talk to me about why you're here...you know where to find me." Without another word, he turned and walked out, closing the door behind him with an easy, soft click.

SURRENDERED II

Did he hear a word she had said?

An hour later, Laura snapped the last suitcase shut and set it roughly on the floor. Everything was ready to go, save the few things they would need in the morning.

She dreaded breaking the news to Andy. She felt disappointed. Fate seemed determined to steal away the life that had ebbed back into him on this trip.

Laura was even willing to admit that she had enjoyed her time here, but she just didn't have coping skills for what she had encountered. Jesse's accusations were too much, and whatever he meant by that last remark about her *reason for being here,* who knew.

She turned off the light and crawled between the smooth cool sheets. Tired and dispirited, she closed her eyes. Jesse's sharp contoured features came uninvited into her vision as she simultaneously felt his lips on her mouth. Not hard and bruising, but gentle and careful. She could see his smoky gray eyes, kind and searching as he kissed her. She scrunched down under the covers and welcomed sleep when it finally came..

The sky was already streaked with rays of earthbound light when Laura woke. Squinting at her watch, she realized she should have been well on her way by this time. *Seven-thirty!* She threw back the covers and vowed to pull out no later than eight o'clock. She and Andy would grab breakfast later.

As soon as she was dressed, she slipped in to wake Andy. She wasn't a bit surprised when she found him gone. His day probably began with a roaring appetite an hour and a half ago.

She decided to load the car, then find him, dreading to break the news to him.

After loading the last suitcase into the back compartment, she clicked the rear door shut, then wheeled around suddenly at the sound of hard pounding hooves approaching the barn across the lane.

"Jesse! You in there?" the excited man yelled.

Laura recognized him as one of the ranch hands.

In a few seconds, Jesse appeared, stopping middle ways of the open barn door. "What's up, Ben?"

"That Parker boy...Dodger ran off with him. Donny's after him, but you better bring the jeep just in case he falls off. Head toward the line shack."

"Oh, no!" Laura sprang across the drive, panic driving her steps as she reached the jeep in unison with Jesse. Still he had to wait for her to scramble in before throwing up a cloud of dust behind them. A couple minutes of silence between them created an electric current that finally demanded an outlet. Laura provided it.

"How could you allow that child to ride out alone? If anything happens to him...if..." Her voice broke up, but the warm hand that was suddenly squeezing her shoulder surprisingly quieted her.

"He'll be all right, Laura. We'll catch up to him...And when we do...I'll take care of it." The authority in Jesse's voice was oddly comforting to her screaming insides, but she didn't trust this man to deal with her child.

She looked at him, realizing that was the first time she'd heard him use her first name. "What do you mean?"

"Just exactly what I said. You're right. This is my fault and I'll handle it my way…Understand?" He glanced at her, a stern line creasing the corners of his mouth, but the worry lined in his brow was obvious.

Laura didn't answer him, but sat stiffly in the open-topped vehicle and held tightly to the edge of the seat and the window frame to keep from being bounced out. The rough pasture ground seemed to go unnoticed to Jesse. He picked up speed, bouncing the jeep over holes and rocks.

A short distance across the open field, Laura could see a horse, then a man a short distance from it stooped low to the ground. The whole picture came into focus. She gasped as she slapped her hand over her mouth. The man was Donny and underneath his bent over frame laid Andy, flat on his back and unmoving.

"Stay here!" Jesse commanded. He stopped the jeep and stepped over the side even before the wheels stopped rolling. Laura ignored him and had to run in order to keep up with his long strides.

"Andy!" She fell to her knees on the opposite side of his little body.

"He's okay, Laura. He's fine." Donny's words sent a blood-drained weakness through her entire body. Her eyes clouded and blurred the wide-eyed little face on the ground. But she could see his expression that clearly said he was not only all right, but enjoying the attention.

"Nothing's broken. He seems to be none the worse for wear. Let's get you on your feet, Pard." Donny gently pulled Andy up and wiped the dust off his back and the seat of his pants.

Laura pulled Andy to her, hugging him, laughing and scolding all in the same breath. A minute later she noticed the two brothers were hovering over Andy's mount. It's legs were folded underneath it, except for one front leg that was protruding out to the side, badly twisted.

Laura got to her feet and stood still, holding onto Andy's shoulder. The cries coming from the downed horse were heartbreaking. She turned away and forcing Andy with her, walked back to the jeep.

After a few minutes, Jesse came striding toward the jeep. Laura was about to ask about the horse, but he walked past her without a glance, then stopped in front of Andy where he sat on the back of the vehicle.

"Why did you ride out of the corral, son?" Jesse spoke with the same calm that smoothed the creases in his face.

The boy tilted his head back to look up at his mountain sized friend, then quickly lowered his face and stared at the ground. "I...I don't know why." He glanced quickly at his mother, then down again. "I just did...that's all."

"You disobeyed me, Andy. And not only me...but your mother. Am I right?"

"Yes sir." He continued to stare at the ground.

Jesse turned and walked a few steps to a thin scrubby little tree. He snapped off a branch and ran his hand down it to strip the leaves off.

Laura was horrified. She stepped out of the jeep and quickly moved in front of Andy. A silent dare riveted the air between her and Jesse.

"Come here, son." Jesse demanded, ignoring Laura's protective move.

"He will not!" she spewed between clinched teeth.

Andy stepped suddenly around his mother to stand in front of her and looked up at her with a sideways glance. "It's okay, Mom...I think I have to." He walked slowly, looking straight at Jesse and stopped directly in front of him.

A sharp pain pierced Laura's heart. She could only stare with her eyes glazed and wide, amazed at her little son. His courage was large for his years. She was proud of his determination to stand alone, to be responsible for his own mistakes, yet it was heartbreaking for her at his tender age. Her *mama* legs wanted to run after him and scoop him up, but her heart knew this was just one of many breaks she would feel as he grew to become a man—as the apron strings began to be cut away.

Unable to hear the words passing between the two, Laura studied Jesse's face, knowing she would be incapable of remaining where she was if he showed a hint of anger toward her son. There was no sign, however. His eyes reflected gentleness as he spoke. She watched Andy nod his head.

Finally, Jesse broke the unused switch in half and tossed it to the ground.

There was a calmness about the pair as they walked back toward her. Frankly, Laura was confused at the slight grin pulling at either side of Andy's mouth, but it lasted only a moment as a loud blast suddenly filled the air. It was a gunshot aimed at the injured horse. Laura couldn't follow Andy's gaze in its direction, but jerked her head back and closed her eyes, furiously fighting the lump in her throat.

When she opened her eyes again, Jesse was staring down into her face. "I'm sorry either of you had to witness that but the pony was in too much agony to make him wait." Their eyes held momentarily and Laura felt something shatter inside herself. His eyes were deep pools of gray, seeming to pierce her heart with a whole new kind of break. She looked away.

"Guess we better load up." Jesse gestured toward the vehicle where Andy was already perched and somberly watching Donny and Ben maneuver the saddle from the dead horse. After tossing the riding tack into the empty back half of the jeep, Donny patted Andy's knee and assured him that if God hadn't needed another mount in Heaven, well, He probably would not have let this happen.

0   The remark sounded strange to Laura. Cowboys talking about God. .

The trio rode in silence the short way back, absorbed in their own thoughts. Laura wondered what had taken the place of the switch Jesse had thrown away. It didn't matter now.

After such a morning, she dreaded springing another disappointment on Andy, but she figured he was bound to have had enough of this trip himself.

Jesse stopped and killed the engine in front of Laura's cabin, then shifted sideways in his seat to look at the boy in the back seat. "Andy, you can start now with those water troughs in the corral. Fill them to the rim. The water faucet is on the other side of the barn.

"Yes, sir!" Andy was over the side and running for the barn, beaming with excitement.

Laura turned suspicious eyes on Jesse. "I seemed to have missed something here."

"Figured I'd get him busy long enough to help you unload those suitcases out of your vehicle."

"I have no intention of unloading those suitcases." She stared at him, defiance shooting blue fire.

"I figured you might object...but I'd suggest you reconsider. Andy has a big lesson to learn after that stunt this morning. He has agreed to work out the damage during the rest of his stay. I gather he hasn't been told of your plans to leave?"

"I've hardly had a chance to tell him."

"Good, then there's no need for an explanation. Unpack. And if for no other reason...give the kid a chance to make good on his choice of punishment. He wants to pay his debt...Let him."

His choice of punishment?

"You gave him a choice of working or...or..." She felt stricken.

"Laura, if I hadn't been positive of what his choice would be...I would not have given him one. This way...I didn't order him to work for me. It was his idea. He offered to pay his debt like a man would." He pointed toward the corral where Andy was laughing and shooting water at a playful red and white spotty dog. "Look at him. He's happy about it...Not to mention Pup."

This was unfair, she thought moodily, turning her head to stare into the thickly set trees. The idea of spending the next couple of weeks with this mountain man accusing her every move galled her. Yet, even so, she felt responsible and heart sick over what had happened to the horse. And even at such a tender age, she knew Andy had to fulfill his agreement to pay for his mistake.

She looked back toward the corral at the sound of the dog barking and her son's squeals. She couldn't help but smile. Andy was laughing.

She turned back around and tauntingly slanted her eyes up at Jesse. "Aren't you afraid two weeks might be enough time for me to corrupt little brother?"

He met her eyes straight on. "I believe that's been understood...all the way around."

She wasn't sure what he meant by that and he gave her no time to inquire as he reached across her, flipped the handle and shoved open the door.

Laura watched as he easily carried all four cases inside and set them inside her bedroom door. The easy way that he carried his tall and muscled frame held her stare for too long. When he turned around and caught her looking, he smiled, unnerving her to the roots of her hair. Her heartbeat jerked out of rhythm a couple of beats and she felt ashamed at what was happening inside of her for a man with brutal tendencies like his. Loneliness. That's all it was.

"Thank you," she stated as matter of fact as she could get out.

His eyes seemed to take on a darker gray pitch as he stared at her. Amusement flickered for an instant. "You know...you might find your stay a little more tolerable if you'd soften up. Your little mouth has a good start already."

Laura felt her face burn. She didn't know what to say. This was a man she didn't know, but was causing her stomach to flip flop like she had a schoolgirl crush on him. He was referring to the kiss she had shared with him. No—that he had forced out of her.

"That's not exactly how it was," she defended herself.

"That's the way it was, lady. Is this a guilt complex you're carrying around?" He moved quickly. Laura stifled a gasp as he took her wrist and raised it, forcing the wedding ring on her finger to within inches of her face. His tone was soft despite his solid grip. "Is that it? Are you still wearing your mourning gear?"

She trembled slightly. She had refused all these months to remove it. The circle of small stones had been a part of her for so long. Tears trickled down her face.

"Why are you doing this?" she choked out a whisper.

"Come here and I'll show you." His tone was kind, but sternly deep. Catching her upper arm, he took her to the opposite side of the room. "There, Laura Parker...Look at yourself." He applied enough pressure to the back of her neck to center her face in the front of a small mirror on the wall.

She looked at her reddened eyes and wet face, then moved her gaze to lock eyes on Jesse's through the glass. She was too shocked at his actions to speak.

He was staring back at her, holding her gaze with an unwavering sternness. "Now you tell me what kind of a future a woman in that condition has to look forward to...much less what she can offer a little boy."

She remained silent, barely breathing in and out.

Turning her around to face him, his hands gently rubbed her shoulders as he attempted to lighten her tension. "Andy's been without his mother long enough" he said quietly.

She jerked her head as though he had hit her. "That's not true. You don't understand what it's like to suddenly have to live...to survive..."

"No...not me. You. Life is way more than just surviving. You don't know what it's like to really live. He's dead, Laura. He's been dead for months and he's never coming back. Andy can't get his dad back...but he's desperate for his mother to come back and live with him."

"Please stop!" she moaned as she slammed her hands over her ears. Hysteria threatened, dizziness crowded her mind as Jesse held a strong grip on her arms.

"No. I won't stop until you realize that you have the responsibility of going on in this life. You have to. That boy of yours is in need of a mother...not an emotional cripple!"

Hysteria took her as she found herself encircled tightly in Jesse's arms, the heat of his strength searing through her weary body. Her heart pounded wildly against his huge warm chest. His gentle prompting eventually calmed her and he settled her on the love seat. He bent over her and lifted her chin to search her eyes deeply for a moment, then straightened and walked slowly out of the cabin.

Sighing, she relished the wave of relief that seemed to give her body a sensation of floating. She laid her head back and closed her eyes, allowing herself to succumb to a placid contentment, something she couldn't remember ever feeling before.

***

CHAPTER THREE

Laura discovered with a start that the morning sun had changed suddenly into a dark thick mass of clouds. She looked at her watch, then looked again, stunned. One o'clock! She had slept for hours.

Hurrying to the window, she looked out. There was no sign of Andy or anyone for that matter. Suddenly large drops of water began splattering against the pane until she couldn't focus through it. Well, she wouldn't get excited. She was certain Andy would be with Donny or Jesse. Possibly he was still in the barn.

She reached for the phone to call headquarters when it rang and startled her. She grabbed it.

"Hello, Mom?"

"Hey, Andy."

"Jesse showed me how to call you. I'm at his house. I'll stay here 'til the rain stops...Can I?"

She chuckled. "Yes...you can, and thanks for calling to ask." She reminded him to mind his manners. "Got that?" she asked to be sure he was still listening.

He didn't answer her, but she knew he was still there. She could hear him breathing. "Andy... hel...lo." Laura couldn't help but smile while she waited through his silence.

"Dodger died." He finally spoke so softly she barely heard him.

It took a few seconds before she remembered. *Dodger ran off with that Parker boy.* The horse. A pang hit her chest.

"Yes, baby...I know."

"Jesse said two legs got broke because he stepped in a hole and...and Dodger couldn't be fixed. He had to go to Heaven with Jesus. But his legs are fixed now. Is Daddy fixed too, Mom? Can they come back now cause they're fixed?"

Laura squeezed her eyes shut, glad she was not face to face with her son at this moment. Her heart was aching for him. She hadn't stopped to think how this morning's tragedy with the horse might have affected him. Maybe Jesse was right. She had been so self-absorbed that she hadn't seen this coming. And she should have. First, his dad. Now, the horse. He was carrying around too heavy a burden for a five year old. And she hadn't realized how heavy until this minute.

"No, honey," she finally managed as evenly as she could. "They...they...can't come back."

"Well, Mom. What do they do up in Heaven?"

She had no idea how to answer him. In fact, she felt very angry at the whole religious idea of some la-la land called

Heaven. She knew some people needed to think that way—about a lovely, singing with angels kind of place where their deceased family went in order to find some acceptance of death. In truth, she didn't believe in an afterlife. You live, then die, then nothing. It angered her that she had no solace for her young son, unless she lied to him.

"I bet Jesse knows more about that than I do, sweetheart. Ask him about Heaven." She hated passing the buck that way, especially having to sidestep a perfectly honest question from her child. But again, she was glad her brain was quick enough to give him an answer that was not a lie and did not break his heart.

"Okay," he said simply and almost happily, then hung up.

After missing breakfast, then lunch, cold sausage and crackers looked like a feast. After steaming a cup of tea, she turned on a small flame in the fire place and settled in on the couch. The food gave her a new surge of physical strength, but in spite of her efforts, oppression ebbed in. The dark gloom outside the window mimicked what she felt. Streaks of lightening laced the dark clouds off in the distance, followed by a soft rumble of thunder. How akin her own circumstances were to the sudden change in weather. Unpredictable.

The morning just past seemed unreal as her mind reviewed it. She felt like a prisoner because of her sense of duty to Andy in these circumstances and because she had been manhandled by an overgrown bully in cowboy boots who seemed to derive some sordid pleasure in throwing her into fits of pain and heartache. His words had been cruel and she had been forced to listen, to hear the same gut wrenching words spoken to her many months ago. *He's dead.*

The words pounded in her mind and she covered her ears with her hands as though that would shut them off. But there were no tears this time. She was amazed at the complacent acceptance that had settled on her; an acceptance that seemed to free her spirit into a new yearning to live and laugh again. The change must have been so gradual that she hadn't realized it was happening.

Laura allowed only a hint of admittance that Jesse could have intended to help her instead of ruthlessly humiliate her. But there was something else on his mind where she as concerned; a strange indefinable look deep in his steely eyes— one she didn't understand at all.

She absently twisted her ring around on her finger, slipping it off, moving it back and forth between her fingers to watch the light cast tiny red and blue twinkles off of the tiny diamonds. Each spark seemed to draw its own memory to the surface of her mind, but they were not particularly welcomed memories. She slipped the ring back on.

The storm passed almost as abruptly as it had started. The sunlight seemed to Laura brighter than she had ever seen it. It was almost blinding, but she was compelled to get outside in the middle of it.

After unpacking again, she exchanged her cotton top for a long sleeve pullover to ward off the cool dampness. And besides, she liked the way it looked on her slender frame.

Outside, she found the thirsty earth had swallowed most of the rain water. Many of the other guests had wandered out for some fresh air. She returned their greetings, but avoided stopping for conversation, as the force of her own thoughts drew her toward a need for privacy.

There wasn't much room for that in the ranch yard, so she slowly made her way down a narrow path that wound itself in and out of big trees, then across a small open field. Funny, she thought, how the rain-sparkled grass and wild flowers looked different. The mixed colors of yellow and red and violet were more beautiful today than she had ever noticed before. For a moment she was almost persuaded to lie down in the middle of them.

She watched with fascination as tiny furry animals of one sort or another scampered and darted through the bursting color. Nature had a spring celebration all its own, one that shouldn't be disturbed or defiled by her silliness. And besides that, she wasn't real excited about taking a mud bath.

A squirrel rustled around the base of a cottonwood tree, stopping at a safe distance to stare at her.

"Hello, little guy," she coaxed, but he raced over to another tree, then climbed up to hide himself in the leafy branches.

Laura leaned against the massive cottonwood and closed her eyes, envisioning herself as a squirrel and spending her days gathering nuts feeling absolutely no concern about past days nor future ones. She smiled at the thought.

"Is this a private joke?"

SURRENDERED II

The sudden masculine intrusion jerked her out of her fairy tale enough that she moved in preparation to run. She was looking up into Jesse's face, slowly realizing that his hand was tightened around her upper arm.

"Whoa... I didn't mean to scare you." She saw humor in his eyes, but laced with a glinting excitement aimed directly at her.

"I...I just didn't know anyone was here." She was trembling, strongly conscious of his hand holding her.

"Walking off the ranch yard like that was a foolish thing to do." His scolding tone didn't match the ardor that feasted on her. He dropped his hand, but remained standing close and Laura found that she had no desire to move away from him.

"Do you make a habit of spying on your guests?" She straightened taller and met his gaze head on.

"Sometimes a watchful eye is necessary."

"And how do you decide who needs watched?" The way he kept looking at her made her blush.

"It's too easy for a lonely young woman to wander into danger," he finally said. The amusement in his eyes was replaced with a deep brooding gray.

Fully aware of what he was insinuating, she couldn't seem to find a good retort. Her heart was pounding like a Cherokee Tom-tom and for the life of her she didn't know why.

"You get a real kick out of bugging me...don't you, Mr. Brandon?" She finally managed to blurt out, deliberately using his formal name.

A crooked grin altered his face, sending a shiver up her back. She felt like slapping it off, and then found herself admiring the handsome roguish appearance of it.

-336 "Is that what I do?" The huskiness in his voice caused her stomach to lurch sending shivers down her legs to her toes. She lowered her eyes quickly unable to hold up under his intense gaze.

"Let me suggest, mam, that the next time you decide to go hiking...try one of the supervised outings. I don't always have the time to spare for rescue operations."

Rescue? Laura jerked her head back in surprise, then anger. "I did not need to be rescued. I walked out here...I can walk back."

His eyes narrowed slightly. "Then let me put that another way. I'm the ramrod of this outfit...which makes me responsible for the safety of the people that come here. I've always taken that responsibility seriously and I'll do whatever is necessary to prevent accidents such as the one that happened this morning. Walking off out here was a little...naïve."

"So that's what this is about. Sounds like us *Parkers* have a trouble making reputation going for ourselves. I'm not a child, Mr. Brandon...and don't you dare try to bully me. Keep your insults to yourself and you can be sure I'll do everything in my power to keep my *stupidity* out of your way. Excuse me!" She turned and headed down the trail, royally ticked off.

Jesse's long strides brought him quickly beside her. He caught her arm and stopped her, then turned her gently around to look at him. A look of contrition on his so masculine face was almost her undoing. Did he know a look like that coming from such brute and brawn would melt a woman in her tracks, even when she's mad?

"I'm sorry, Laura."

Those words came out like a soft caress. If he meant to shock her, he did. If he meant to remind her of the roughness of his face against hers or the kiss that she had almost drowned in, he did.

His eyes held no mockery, no harshness as he continued. "I wasn't trying to insult you. Naïve does not mean stupid...far from it. You just seem to have a very sheltered innocence about you." He turned his head and shot her a flattering sideways glance that was meant to lighten the moment. "It's kinda nice and I like it."

Suddenly he dropped his hand from her arm and motioned in the direction of the ranch. "I think we'd better get back to the crowd before I forget myself."

Her legs weakened as she looked up at him. His expression held an emotion that she could read, one that said he meant exactly what he'd implied, but his quick-change held her in a still, quiet shock. Her brain urged her to go, but not seriously enough.

They stood silent for a long moment. She was so aware of his big frame looming over her, his hot breath bathing her face until suddenly she felt his hands pulling her against him. Then he was kissing her, gently at first, then like a starving man, the kiss deepened into such as she had not experienced in her life.

Matt had been her only lover and romance was not one of his strong concerns. As out of the blue as this moment had happened, pangs of guilt tore at her just as suddenly when she felt the tight pressure of her wedding ring biting into her finger and overwhelming her emotions. She pushed against his chest with both hands and he jerked his head back, but wrapped her wrists tightly with his long fingers. Her heart was in her throat.

"Why is this wrong," she whispered, speaking mainly to herself?

He pulled on her wrists to still her and force her to look up at his face. His eyes were dark with passion. "This is *not* wrong, Laura. Nothing about you or your need to be loved is wrong...Not *one* thing."

He slowly let go of her and took a half step back. His slamming heartbeat told him to back off. Some sense of possession seemed to have taken him over where Matthew's wife and son were concerned. Standing apart from her seemed to sober him up enough to give her a gentle nudge on her shoulder to point her back down the cow trail she'd walked out here on.

"Hike back up that trail and don't slow down until you reach the ranch yard." His command was more for himself now than for her. His stomach was clenched up in a hard knot. He tried not to think about what was happening to him again. He shook his head to clear it from the irrational joy that wanted to overtake him. Heaven help, he was falling for this woman. His best friend's wife. Matthew's widow.

He watched her slender form move with purpose across the open field, never glancing back at him once. He drew a deep shuddering breath and slowed down enough to let her reach the cover of the trees and disappear from his view.

Laura continued her fast pace, knowing Jesse was purposefully hanging back to let her find her own way back to her cabin. Once inside, she stood with her back against the closed door, still feeling the imprint of Jesse's lips on hers.

She hadn't been much more than a child when she married Matthew and had more or less settled into an acceptance of the physical part of married life. Oh, she had, in time, learned to give and receive the pleasures of sex with her husband, but she was only now realizing that he had consumed every area of her life, including the strength of their lovemaking. This was a part of her that had not truly been fulfilled. She was beginning to realize that there was more to this part of her life than she had yet experienced.

For the first time since Matt's death, Laura desperately wanted her freedom. She wanted released from the emotional imprisonment that her ghetto upbringing and youthful marriage had come with.

She shook the rambling thoughts aside and began listening to the noises outside. From the open window, she watched the other guests, some standing in groups of two or three talking, children running and playing. She caught sight of Andy's towhead bent over where he was kneeling in the wet dirt with a couple of other small boys shooting a concentrated game of marbles.

She wondered if she was doing right, allowing this stranger to punish Andy. But oddly enough, he appeared happier than he'd been in months. The few chores he had, he whistled while he worked. So what was she worried about? Maybe she was a little envious of the ease in which children handled the rougher edges of life.

The supper bell clanged suddenly and Laura was starved. Andy and his new friends jumped up and ran for the chuck wagon. He caught sight of her peeking out the window as he went by.

"Come on, Mom. Time to eat!" he yelled, motioning her out with a wave of his arm, never missing a step.

Laura ran her fingers through her hair, then swung open the door, and let it slam behind her. She was surprised at the spring in her steps. She made up her mind to lighten up and enjoy.

The chow line was long by the time she stepped in place, but she enjoyed small talk with the other guests while she waited. One young woman who stood behind Laura was particularly interesting. She was taller than Laura, very slim with tight jeans tucked into knee high riding boots. She looked around Laura's age.

"Hi. Betsy Wilkins. They just call me Bett around here," she said, smiling.

"I'm glad to meet you, Bett. I'm Laura Parker." Laura didn't remember seeing her before.

"Isn't this place gorgeous? I love springtime at High Point. It's always so beautiful." Bett bubbled with the delight of a kid.

"Oh, then you've been here before?" Laura asked, more interested.

"Three years to the month," a masculine voice came from behind Laura's head. She watched, strangely breathless, as he walked around her and extended his arm, settling it around Bett's shoulders. "And not long enough...as far as I'm concerned," he added.

The look and smile exchanged between the pair gave Laura a sinking feeling. She let out a breath, not realizing she had been holding it.

Jesse put his mouth close to Bett's ear and hugged her a little closer. "Eat light. I've got a little time for that ride you wanted this evening...and we both know what a horseback ride can do to a full stomach."

Bett laughed up at him, her eyes flashing an understanding of what was evidently a private joke. "Suppose we cut the chow line and eat afterward."

"Suits me," Jesse agreed.

"Laura..." Jesse looked straight at her, but nothing in his face gave a hint that he even remembered the earlier incident between them, "you'll be at the big shindig tonight...won't you?"

"Sure she will," Bett answered for her. "Everybody's invited. It's a pre-wedding celebration. Isn't that what you called it, Jesse?"

"Yeah...something like that," he answered, but his eyes were fixed curiously on Laura.

Imagine that!

Laura set her eyes on the young woman, hoping she was coming across with a festive innocence. "Of course I'll come.

Thanks for the invitation." Why were her knees trying to buckle?

"Good. See you around eight...on the pavilion. Come on, Jesse...we're burnin daylight." She grabbed his shirtfront, pulled and giggled like a teenager.

Laura attempted a smile and waved them off. *I hope he falls and breaks both lips,* she seethed. Her raging appetite went sour several minutes ago. But it was her turn to take a plate, so she numbly went through the motions. As she walked toward the tables and chairs near the pavilion, the lights popped on to reveal the balloons and ribbons and tables all decorated for a party. She sat, numbly wondering what she would do with all this food on her plate. It wasn't going to fit past the lump in her throat.

A wedding? My God, couldn't he have told her. A last hoorah. That's what had happened between her and Jesse. Nothing more. She struggled in her mind to force the situation into proper perspective. The man was hardly more than a stranger and a kiss or two shared between them didn't mean a thing. Obviously. But it did mean that a new yearning, a desire had been awakened in her by those meaningless kisses, those heavy, strong arms holding her close and warm. Jesse had brought her out of her seclusion of mourning and made her want to live again. Really live. She could be thankful for that and move on forward now, she and Andy.

She waited for her mental resolve to delete the image of the impeccable figure of the big woodsy cowboy with black silken hair, gray piercing eyes. But it did not.

Above the voices and laughter in the ranch yard rang the sound of music. The band was already starting to play and Laura had not convinced herself she could do this tonight. She had almost had to arm wrestle Andy to get him bathed and he fell sound asleep before she could get him into more clothes to go out again. Her body was calling for a rest as well. But mostly her heart was heavy.

No matter how firmly she resolved to let go of Jesse Brandon, she failed. He had imprinted himself on the inner pictures of her mind, replacing the trauma of her husband's physical death with a different hurt in her heart.

She had let herself become emotionally tangled with a dead-end situation. But wasn't that where she stood before she came here? Nothing had really changed. She was still Laura Parker, still widowed, still unsure of what life would throw at her around the next corner.

She should go to the party. Why not? Beats sitting in this cabin analyzing her dying heart over and over. She would enjoy the music and watching the dancers. After freshening her makeup and sliding her fingers through her hair, she checked on Andy one more time.

It was dark outside, but the naturally pleasant night sounds couldn't be heard over the country music that rolled through the black space. Only a faint stream of light bounced over the top of the barn to break the darkness so she could see to walk. The chilly air still held a lingering freshness from the earlier rain and it felt good as it gently whispered through her blonde layers.

The assumption that she might observe the festivities in an inconspicuous manner was short lived as her appearance near the pavilion was spotted by the younger Brandon, who happened to be true to form this evening. Laura's protest went unheeded as Donny swung her onto the dance floor and rested his hands around her waist. His wide, loose-legged two-step kept her mind occupied trying to keep up with him. When the music stopped, she was breathless and laughing and thoroughly glad she had come. She joined the applause, stealing a glance around to be sure her boots and jeans fit everyone else's attire. Children ran onto the pavilion, weaving in and out of lingering couples waiting for the next song.

Laura also noticed that Jesse was nowhere in sight and neither was Bett. Were they still riding? She could imagine what they were doing out in the woods in the dark. Did it matter? She had to keep her mind on herself and Andy and the fact that the evening was young and so was she.

A half hour later found her seated at Donny's table and out of breath. The place certainly wasn't short on dancing partners, at least not of the male species. She hadn't danced with the same man twice. Even Cook waltzed her around the floor with the gentle expertise of a professional. Hank Walton, she had managed to get Cook's real identity out of him, wasn't big on conversation, but his camp cooking was excellent and his dancing ability was a surprise. She decided if he was too shy to return for an encore, she would look him up herself.

SURRENDERED II

Laura felt exhilarated at being able to open up and let loose a little. As a child, she was given to mischievousness. Pressured by her early marriage and subdued lifestyle, that she hadn't realized *was* so subdued until now, she had withdrawn from truly enjoying life. But it was time now to spread her wings again and explore her freedom.

A new rush of childish exuberance brought her to her feet. She grabbed Donny's shirt sleeve and pulled him to his feet and onto the dance floor.

"That's my girl!" he exclaimed. "Dancin' at these shindigs is just like eatin' tater chips…One just won't cut it."

They laughed as he grasped her around the waist and whirled her into an easy glide, passing the other dancers with his long strides.

Laura had to wonder how Donny could be such a drastic contrast to his older brother. Certainly her stay at this ranch would be easier to handle with this sweet kid around. *His majesty* could read whatever he liked into her relationship with his brother. He was full of fun and she was enjoying it.

On the last note of the song, he pushed Laura's arm above her head and whirled her full circle several times before catching her to him to stop her. He planted a quick kiss on her cheek for good measure.

"Hello, big brother!" Donny spoke through his laughter, as he looked behind Laura. "I wondered where you got off to. The fun's just starting."

Laura jerked around, stunned at Jesse's sudden appearance on the floor.

"So I see," came his dry retort as he stared hard at Laura.

Her eyes wide, she met his stony gaze head on.

"So...how was your ride?" She glanced around but saw no sign of Betsy. Without waiting for an answer, she nervously asked, "Where's Bett? A pre-wedding bash should call for two honored guests."

The way Jesse was staring hard at her, she knew she hadn't done a good job of hiding herself. He seemed to be looking straight through her now, debating something.

"Dance with me." His voice was gravelly in her ear. It was a command and before she could walk away and leave him snubbed, she found herself being rudely dragged against his towering frame. The music was a slow two-step, but her pulse jumped into pandemonium.

"I do not want to dance with you, Mr. Brandon!" She jerked backward but the crook of his arm was secured around her waist forcing her body to sway against his to the music.

"Loosen up, Ms. Parker. I'd think you'd at least have the manners to oblige your host." The glare of gray steel also held a spark of laughter, serving to throw her anger into high gear.

"And what do you suppose the bride-to-be would have to say about this? I could fill her in on a few details that would blow a hole right through this little pre-wedding party."

"Bett?" He glanced off for a minute then looked back at her, his expression unreadable. He slowly lifted the corner of his mouth in some kind of cocky amusement. He appeared ready to say something, but changed his mind, fixing a firm set to his jaw. After a cool minute, he told her, "Bett's mother got sick... and she had to leave this evening. I would suggest, first of all, that you cool off and forget about blabbing a lot of nonsense to her."

The song ended, but he held her tight in the middle of the dance floor, disregarding the curious looks from the people around them. "And second..." his eyes were flashing again as he grasped her chin and forced her face up to his. "I don't like being threatened. Don't forget it."

He released her, but she was too stunned to move away from him. He said, in a calmer tone, "Now that that's understood... there's another matter I want to discuss with you. Come to my office at headquarters at eight o'clock tomorrow morning." He turned and strode off into the darkness.

His arrogance was superior to any she had encountered in her life! At some point, he was sure to meet up with a pompous, high-handed chauvinist bigger than himself. *Just let me be around for the show!!*

Her stewing was brought down to a simmer as Hank appeared with an arm outstretched, his feet already scooting in time to the music. They waltzed and she was glad this time that he wasn't much on conversation.

She found it impossible to concentrate on anything but tomorrow morning. What could Jesse want with her that he couldn't spit at her right then? Maybe he wanted to make sure she wouldn't actually reveal his two-timing to Bett. Could she have gotten to the big bad Brandon, after all?

That thought lightened her mood somewhat. Then another possibility struck her. He may have decided to relieve Andy of his punishment early and send them packing to ensure his safety. That had to be it and she would make sure he had the opportunity to do so, and on time!

In spite of everything, Laura was anxious to get on with the meeting with Jesse. The muscles in her legs were not happy campers after the hours of dancing the night before, but her step was light as she walked up the steps at headquarters. She absently envisioned the big house with a new paint job, then smiled, thinking how much it was like it's owner. He could use a good *fixing up*, too.

"A-plus for promptness," Jesse said. His deep male voice startled her from behind the darkened screen door. He pushed it and held it open for her to come inside. "I won't even ask what that smile was about...but I'm glad to see it's genuine," he said cheerfully.

Oh, it's genuine, all right. She stepped past him into the wide hallway, avoiding his eyes. His mood was strangely lighthearted, one that was brand new to her, but she didn't look up to view it more closely. He took her elbow lightly and ushered her down the hallway without any further word, then through a large solid wood door off to the left.

The office was much like the exterior of the house. In bad need of a face lift. The room was definitely a masculine hovel with an old beat up dark oak desk boxed in by old dark wall paneling. Bamboo shades slightly lighter than dark covered the two windows on the far wall, one of them rolled part way up to let in some sunlight. A small antique looking settee was positioned a few feet in front of the desk with a small, round glass-topped table next to it holding a lamp and an ashtray.

Her eyes scanned the inset shelving that covered one wall. Books lined most of the lower shelves, the higher ones were empty. Laura had always loved books and wished for a fleeting second that she was alone to look through them.

She turned her attention to Jesse and found him looking at her with a questioning lift in his brows. He motioned her to the little settee, then sat at his desk. Their glances locked for several seconds, then he smiled, taking Laura aback.

Now she knew she had him over a barrel and she was even more certain that he was desperate to keep her mouth closed. She couldn't see Jesse Brandon begging her silence, so he had to have another way in mind. For a minute, she was almost prepared to insist on her full two weeks, just to watch him squirm.

"I have a business proposition."

Her mind jerked out of its mischievous rambling.

"I'll get right to the point. As you already know...Betsy Wilkins had to leave last night and won't be returning...Not to work that is. That leaves me without a secretary. I'm offering you the job for as long as you're here. I'll pay one month's salary in advance. I'll need you three or four hours each day."

Shocked, Laura stared at him, wordless. He waited, letting her digest his offer.

"But...I...I don't have proper clothes." That was all she could think of to say.

His laugh held a note of merriment, curiously mixed with a challenge for her. "If that's all you're worried about...then there's no problem. Boots and jeans fit in around here just fine. You'll still have most of the day to enjoy the activities."

"But...I don't have a month...And I have Andy. I don't think..."

"Between Donny and myself, Andy will feel like top dog out there...and you'll be free to leave whenever you choose. At least I'll have time to find a permanent replacement." He picked up a sheet of paper on his desk and took it to her. "Unless the answer is 'no'...I'd like you to fill this out for me. You can bring it back after lunch...around one o'clock. You can start then."

Had her mind not been thrown into such stupor, she would have objected to his pushing and making up her mind for her. She was certain he was playing some sort of game, and decided she'd be wise to not under estimate the man.

His hand pressed to her back a minute later guided her down the hall and out the door. "One o'clock," he reminded her, as she went down the steps.

How had this happened, she chided herself as she entered her cabin? She had been prepared to begin packing her bags for home. Instead, here she was, launched on a short course in dude ranching.

Temporary insanity. That's where she had been the past few days. Coming to this barnyard for a vacation, even though she had found a serenity and beauty here, was proof enough that she wasn't thinking clearly from the beginning. And

Jesse's kisses, the feelings he had awakened in her, even raised from the dead, letting the big brute order her around like a child in his care. And he was engaged to be married! And now he had taken over her son as if Andy belonged to him, and put her in his own house, working for him.

This couldn't have happened to her without her consent. It was the kiss. It was the strong arms of an attractive man holding her close, making her feel things inside herself that she had never felt in her life. Not even with Matthew.

Right now all she could manufacture for Jesse was disgust for the way he had seen fit to belittle and threaten her last evening, not to mention using her for one last ego inflation before tying the knot.

Even though she had threatened to *tattletale* to Bett, she knew she wouldn't hurt the girl that way. It might save her a heart ache later on, but Laura wasn't willing to go that far. She hardly knew Bett, or Jesse for that matter. Let them find their own way.

There was usually a bright side to everything. At least this would give her a few hours a day to work and pass away the time she and Andy had left. Knowing Jesse had charge of most of the activities, he would be out with the *dudes* most of the day. Score one for her!

She spent the remainder of the morning on a hiking trip with Andy, headed up by one of the ranch hands she hadn't seen before.

The lunch bell clanged just as they returned. Laura chalked up her lack of appetite to the exhausting walk, but knew her *dude ranching 101* with Jesse in about an hour was more the cause than the hike was.

She forced herself to swallow half of a pimento cheese sandwich and a glass of lemonade while explaining her new job to Andy. He didn't show much interest one way or the other. His little mind was working on one track, as usual.

A group had been rounded up for a wagon ride to the river to fish all afternoon and Andy was front and center on the buckboard driver's seat. Despite everything else happening here, Laura knew this trip was going to be a hallmark event in her son's life.

***

CHAPTER FOUR

Laura was glad when she walked into the office and found herself alone. The desk was strewed with papers, but she didn't dare review their contents. Instead, she decided it would be all right to thumb through a few books while she waited. Her eyes skimmed the perfectly even rows until she caught sight of a book binding that seemed familiar. She slipped a finger in and pulled it part way out, then a faint stir caused her to look behind her. She hadn't heard Jesse come in, but the way he was standing above her, his feet parted slightly, powerful looking and devastatingly sexy, caused her heart to flutter. She forgot the book, leaving it pulled out.

"Nervous?" He asked, a slight grin creasing the corner of his mouth.

"Actually... one o'clock came and went. I was just...killing time." She raised her eyebrows and looked at her watch for emphasis.

"Point taken." He turned and walked to his desk, all business, and proceeded to explain what to do with the guest information forms, and how to use the calendar to make new reservations.

"Priority is the telephone. Here is a brochure to help you remember what we have to offer and all pertinent information people will want to know. If questions arise that you can't answer...offer to call them back later with the answer. Then talk to me...Simple as that. Now. Do you have any questions before I go?"

The man couldn't get any more all business if he worked at it! Laura found it hard to concentrate on his instructions with the havoc his presence was creating in her. She knew he could handle his manners with the other guests, particularly Betsy. *That* she could understand. But she seemed to be brought up short at every turn. Even at that, she had to work to not look at his full sexy lips and remember how they felt touching hers. Devouring hers.

She realized that she had only heard a bit and piece of his instructions when he stood looking at her as if he expected her to respond to something he'd said. The mocking purse of his lips said he knew she wasn't listening.

He muttered something about saddling some horses, then left without another word.

She seated herself behind the massive desk and flipped through the forms and pamphlets to familiarize herself with the workings of a dude ranch. If anyone called wanting information, she could just read them the brochure. She pulled open the heavy bottom drawer of the desk and pulled out a folder labeled *Documents*. Might be something here to help her sound a little less *dudish* to a new customer. She thumbed through the various papers, not particularly understanding what she read.

Her eyes skimmed past a familiar group of words. She backed up and read again slowly, suddenly feeling as though she couldn't catch a breath. She read *Matthew Ward Parker*. The folder it was in slipped unnoticed to the floor as she held the corner of the document between clenched fingers. She sucked a deep breath and skimmed down the page hurriedly and read *Jesse Dane Brandon*. Jesse Dane Brandon, she repeated in her mind until a rippling shock wave threatened to strangle her. "J.D.," she said aloud, but it came out in a coarse whisper.

It was some minutes before she could pull herself together. Agonizingly slow, the pieces were beginning to fall into place. She recalled the odd feeling, the impression of knowing something peculiar was flowing between herself and Jesse. Now the meaning was becoming horribly clear.

Her head shot up as she remembered the book she left sticking part way out on the self. She raced the few steps across the room and jerked it out, then sunk to the floor holding the book between trembling hands as the document she carried fell to her lap. Without opening its pages, she knew it was one of only a dozen copies of Matt's collection of poetry. She had always thought it a waste of precious talent to allow only a select few to possess this book, but the copies were made as special gifts. His friend, J.D., had been one of those few, she remembered. She opened the cover page and found Matt's signature and a personal inscription to his friend.

Laura thought back to those frustrating weeks she had spent listening to Matt talk about throwing in with J.D. and building a ranch.

She picked up the paper from her lap and reread it. It was right here in black and white. This explained the brochure to this ranch she'd found mixed in with Matt's personal things in his desk.

Laura stared unblinking for several seconds. Her heart began pounding in anger at the possibility that Matt could still throw her world off center, even from the grave. There was a good possibility he was part owner of this ranch. She gathered her wits, deciding she would find out what he had actually done here before saying anything to Jesse.

After replacing the book, she walked back to the desk and replaced the folder and its contents.

Marshall Baines would be a good place to start. He had been Matthew's lawyer before she was even in the picture.

After only a few minutes, she replaced the receiver on the hook. He hadn't enlightened her on any specifics, but admitted he had handled a transaction for Matt some time ago on a property deal in Wyoming. He insisted she come in to see him and he would elaborate the details for her then. But she had heard all she needed to for the time being. Matthew had talked of buying into partnership with J.D. Obviously that's exactly what he had done.

Jesse had known who she was from the beginning and evidently thought she was here to stake a claim. He would never believe she knew nothing about this and that sheer fate had landed her and Andy here.

Well, what did she care what Jesse Brandon thought? She didn't want anything that belonged to the man, but what belonged to Matt was legally hers now and she would have to claim it, if only for Andy's sake.

She closed her eyes and breathed deep, pulling her thoughts together. She wouldn't announce her find just yet. She had the feeling Jesse was playing some type of game with her and this knowledge she had just acquired put her a jump ahead on the playing board. The thought of being on a more equal ground sent a ripple of childish devilment down her spine. *Where in the world did that come from?* Something so different was happening to her lately. Something was waking up inside of her, coming alive. It was a youthful giddiness and she liked the feel of it.

A quarter of an hour later found Laura in her cabin gazing out the window as her thoughts ran like a swift stream. This day had been quite an experience. Maybe she should march over to Jesse and inform him of her discovery. Most likely he would want to buy her out. Then a wicked thought shot through her mind. She laughed aloud as she imagined his reaction to her insisting on running the ranch as an equal owner.

Turning from mental ramblings, she walked to the square framed mirror hanging slightly lopsided on the wall, righted it and stared at herself. What she saw was different, or so it seemed, from the woman that had always stared back at her before. The eyes appeared brighter, a careless glint sharpening the color. She liked what she saw and realized that just possibly she was waking from months, maybe from years of oppression and into a welcomed youthful freedom. With this realization, she felt a sense of excitement at making a game out of this situation with Jesse. She had a weapon now. She just needed to figure out how she would wield it.

Laura mingled with the guests through supper that evening. Andy's fishing tales were full of excitement as he held his own against the stories of some of the older men. There was hardly a person on the place he couldn't call by name.

She hadn't run into Jesse all evening and he was nowhere in sight when she reported for work the next morning. It was just as well. She had a few plans of her own to fulfill during her morning work hours.

First of all, the office, *her* office, could use a little sprucing up. Rearranging, maybe. It was half hers, in all likelihood. Anyway, what did a man know about decorating a room? This one was definitely done in *man drab*. *Early* man drab!

Laura spent the morning at one of her favorite past times. Interior decorating. There wasn't a whole lot she could do with so little to work with, but in between phone calls, *that's really all this job amounted to,* she put a facelift on the ranch office. The filing cabinet was too heavy to move, but the desk slid across the room easy enough with all the girl muscle she could put into it. She found it a much more cheery home in front of the room's only window.

After taking in the room as a whole for a few silent minutes, she visualized the dark paneled walls painted a light shade of tan to open up the dungeon feel. The floor was well-worn hardwood, but a good buff job and an area rug in an Indian red color and design would ranch it up beautifully.

The phone jangled, popping her back to the reason she was in this office anyway. She explained the program to a possible new family of dudes, hung up, then looked up from behind the desk at the new angle of the room's furnishings. *Wow.* Sitting around waiting for dudes to call, she'd let her imagination run amuck. *Jesse will probably consider feeding me to the coyotes when he sees this!* She smiled.

Her gaze moved around the room. So what, if he doesn't like it. She liked it. He hadn't been up front with her since she got here. And that was a mild way of putting it.

"Wow!" That seemed to be her byword for the day. She scooted back in the swivel office chair and let her mind roll over the possibility that half of this ranch—*oh my stars*—could actually belong to her. Suddenly that revelation wanted to be a real brain full. In fact, there could be no other explanation. None. She cut her eyes up, then down the dark walls and wondered where she might get her hands on a bucket or two of happy, cheery paint!

She spied a step stool beside the ceiling high bookcase and began removing dusty pictures and plaques from high up on the walls around the room. A star shaped ornament hung above the doorway right up against the ceiling and too high for her to reach from the stool. She pulled the thickest book she could find from the bookcase wall, placed it in the center of the stool and carefully stood on it. Perfect. Just as she pulled the fairly heavy cast iron star off of the nail it hung on, the door to the office pushed open about half way before it bumped the stool. Laura screamed as her feet wobbled, then the book slid out from under her shooting her sideways into the air.

The corner of her eye caught the huge body form in the doorway just as she crashed to the floor. But the floor wasn't flat and solid. She had fallen on a lump of something. Before she could get her bearings, a loud "ah...crap!" bounced off of her eardrum. Then she realized that the lump was not only beneath her but in process of rolling her off the top of itself as well. And that lump was groaning like it was about to give birth.

She rolled opposite from all the whimpering, then rose up to see Jesse on the floor holding the top of his head, blood oozing between his fingers.

"Oh, no! Jesse!" She realized then that he had dove through the half opened door to break her fall. So much blood. What did he hit his head on? "Jesse?"

He sat up, but kept his head tilted to keep the blood from running down his neck. "Go in the bathroom and get towels, Laura."

Her feet took flight out into the hallway and found the bathroom only one door down. Within a few seconds, she returned and wrapped a wet towel around his head, then helped him to the small sofa now setting against a wall.

Despite the pain in his head and shoulder, Jesse took in the surroundings of the office. Then furious eyes glared into hers before he checked out his head injury a little closer. The bleeding had nearly stopped, but he could feel a lump growing.

When she tried to take a look, he put up an elbow to stop her. "It's fine...There's more blood than injury." He nodded toward an object on the floor. "Is that what you hit me with?"

Laura opened her mouth to refute his ridiculous statement when she saw the cast iron star lying on the floor right about where Jesse's head had been. Her hand went to her open mouth. "Oh no. I...you..."

"Well, I guess that's a start." He muttered. "After I get myself cleaned up...you can start again and tell me what went on in here today." He got up, still pressing the towel against his head. Before taking a step, he eyed her up and down with a surprising look of concern. "Are you hurt?"

The unexpected tenderness in his voice went straight into her heart. She couldn't remember ever hearing such sincerity for her welfare directed at her that way. She just shook her head. In truth, she hadn't felt any pain up to this point, but figured she'd find a sore spot later.

He walked past her and out the door just as the phone rang, making her jump. Just seconds before she finished explaining the dude ranch program once more, Jesse returned wearing a clean shirt, his hair wet and smelling like shampoo. She watched him set the overturned stool upright, then retrieve the book and toss it onto the settee. His gaze moved around the room again, this time more slowly, then fell back on Laura.

She managed to find her voice, but had to strain to make it sound even. "How do you like it?"

He couldn't stop his eyes from rolling. *She did not just ask me that!* "Would we be talking about the sudden lack of blood in my body or the home improvement program you've obviously implemented while I was out?" He smeared at her.

She bristled. "Well...you don't have to be so sarcastic."

"Forgive me...I'm in a little pain here...Not quite myself." He was talking through gritted teeth now. He picked the star up off the floor and handed it to her. "Crawling up on that stool with a slippery book on it was stupid. You could have broken your neck."

"Maybe I was just...naïve."

"No...that was stupid."

"Well...I was in perfect control until you shoved that door against me."

He sighed heavily, rubbed the back of his neck and went out into the hall. Laura watched as he gathered up scattered mail, then his hat.

She was beginning to feel a little guilty about his head ache, until he dumped the load of mail on the desk and began skimming over the reservation calendar. Business as usual.

Without glancing up, he muttered, "If you can find time...I'll show you what to do with this mail."

So he was going to ignore all her arduous work. Sooner or later he would have to notice. She hadn't even started yet!

She sat behind the desk and this time, paid close attention to his instruction, even jotting down a few notes. The jangle of the phone interrupted the lesson, giving her a minute to absorb what he had shown her.

As he reached around behind her to answer the call, his tall frame towered above her, encircling her as he left his free hand resting on the opposite side of the desk.

As much as she tried to ignore it, the closeness sent ripples down her spine. Her mental and physical parts couldn't seem to get their act together. Maybe because most of the time he was a callous, ego shrouded, two-timing Judas. And then he had to go give her, *what,* a look that no man had ever aimed at her before. Eyes that were brimmed with concern for her welfare. One tiny little look that she'd remember for the rest of her life.

OMG! She really needed to get out more. She would have to get hold of this craziness and decided it would all pass. The man had forced himself on her. He had used her to sort of kiss his single life good-bye. He had been heavy handed with her son. Of course her emotions would be nuts.

Matthew had always held a tight rein on her, deciding what she needed whether physically or emotionally and filling those needs almost systematically. But what she was experiencing with Jesse was way different. She had to sort through and deal with her own needs, feelings and desires—alone. She had to control them, decide what was best for her and her son. It suddenly seemed to her that she had not had a true, honest day of her own in her entire life. Maybe she hadn't been able to think for herself before. She was always willing enough to let Matt do it for her. Well, this man would be married soon anyway, and at least that would solve some of this rude awakening she was having.

Jesse replaced the phone receiver and moved to the end of the desk. "Let's wrap this up for today. The answering machine can take the calls."

She cleared the desktop, then looked up to find him eyeing her with some sort of amused expression.

"I'd like you to accompany me into town this evening. Can you be ready by six?"

"Can I at least know where I'm going?"

"No. Just wear your best clothes...Six o'clock." He turned and walked out, leaving her staring with her mouth open.

It took a few minutes to connect with the realization that the great ranch lord had just bullied an order at her—again. That was not an invitation and there wasn't a snowball's chance that she would be going anywhere with him.

Most of the afternoon was spent horseback in the corral with Andy. He was determined she would learn to ride a horse like everyone else. To her surprise, she was enjoying herself, but the moment she dismounted and took a step, she could have sworn she was dragging somebody else's butt behind her. She had heard of saddle sore before, but now she was wearing it. Walking as near perfect as she could stand, she made it to her cabin and a very hot shower before she let herself moan out loud.

After a sweet quarter of an hour soaking her bruised body, she slipped into a loose cotton wrap and stretched out on the love seat. *Ah, blessed rest for weary bones.* She'd never make a good cowgirl at this rate. And even *that* rate was cut short when Jesse Brandon brazenly opened her front door and stepped inside. And dressed to the living hilt!

Her gaze went from his gleaming silver Stetson to his white long sleeved pearl snap western shirt that was belted into dress khaki pants, belt buckle glittering with rows of tiny diamonds. What she could see of black cowboy boots shined almost clear. Slowly her eyes moved back up until a pair of gray darts paralyzed her, except for her heart that was running in overdrive.

Jesse folded his arms across his chest. "It's six o'clock," he stated as if he expected that revelation to send her running for her evening gown, which she didn't have.

"And?"

"And you're not dressed yet."

She stared at him as blankly as she could. "And?"

He let his gaze move to the opposite side of the cabin, then dropped his arms to his sides.

Raising herself up to a sitting position, she watched his lithe, lean form swagger across the room and disappear around the corner. In a second, the light in her bedroom streamed into the tiny hallway.

Shock at the man's audacity held her in place as she listened to the rustling of clothes and hangers. And whistling! He was rummaging through her intimate space and whistling Yankee Doodle! In another few seconds, he reappeared with a pair of beige slacks, the only dress pants she brought, and a black and white chiffon pull over blouse. Still on hangers, he draped them across the back of the sofa.

"Now...if you're not in these clothes and out the door in five minutes flat...I *will* turn the job of dressing you into a twosome." Jesse casually laid down the challenge, but his eyes were piercingly sharp.

Laura couldn't respond immediately. Irritation was building into pure angry disbelief at the arrogance of this big bully, but with her mouth wide open, she struggled to find her voice.

"I...have...have you forgotten that I have a child?" She sucked a deep breath to control the rioting in her mind. "I can't...I *won't* go with you...I never agreed to go out with you."

"I've made arrangements for Andy. He'll be with Donny while we're gone. And...I didn't ask you to go out with me. You owe me this one and the time has come to pay up. Four minutes. I'll wait for you in the jeep." He casually sauntered out and clicked the door shut behind him.

She stared at the closed door, slightly alarmed, but more curious. She hastily dressed, knowing Jesse had all the nerve necessary to come back and help her out. Even though she had heard all her life what curiosity did to the cat, she knew that's what was moving her right now. Where was he taking her?

A full ten minutes later, Laura stepped up into the jeep, surprised at the gentlemanly way Jesse had stepped quickly around to her side and opened the door for her. After pulling out of the ranch onto the highway, he never looked at her. But she hadn't missed the way his slightly hooded eyes had taken in every inch of her when she walked from the cabin to the jeep.

Now, she couldn't take her gaze from him, from admiring his tall form, comfortable behind the wheel of his old ranch jeep, his clean, but work roughened hands competent at jamming gears with the stick shift on the floor. So roguishly handsome.

A short time later, Jesse pulled the jeep into a gravel parking lot beside a small, very old white clapboard church. Lots of cars and pickups were jammed into the small parking area. She was confused until she spotted a small compact car parked beside the front door with all the obvious signs. *JUST MARRIED* was printed in bright red lipstick across the back windshield.

The wedding! Laura's jaw dropped at the same time she shot him a dirty look that was meant to kill him dead. He had dragged her to his wedding ceremony.

"I guess this is your sick way of finishing off your last hoorah," she seethed at him. "Well...we'll see who has the last one." Nothing would stop her now from pursuing this property situation. This man would get every *book* she could legally put together thrown right in his arrogant face!

He arched his eyebrows in a gesture of mock confusion, but he didn't bother to look at her or try to conceal the slight smile that pulled one side of his mouth. "Get out...Ms. Parker...You're making me very late."

It dawned on her then that he was standing outside holding her door open. She never saw him get out.

She was trembling, not sure if she could walk once she stood up. She didn't trust herself to speak, but pride alone forced her to dig deep for strength and ignore the brawn and brass...*oh yeah, they were brass, all right*—walking her through the chapel doors. Fervently she wished she were back in the city right now. She wished she'd never left it.

Jesse deposited her on a pew just inside the door. That she was thankful for. At least she wouldn't have to hear all his vows of love and devotion to his new bride. She just hoped he had left her the jeep keys.

She should have time to poke around all she wanted to with Jesse off honeymooning. Get all her ducks in a row about this ranch. But there was no sense of excitement in that now. Or in anything else for that matter. There was only a fullness that had formed in her throat. She tried to breathe deeply enough to open up the blockage, but how do you swallow a tangled up emotional knot? How could she have attached herself to Jesse Brandon this fast? How could her heart so suddenly feel like it was shattering in a million pieces? It shouldn't matter to her that Jesse was about to be married. But it did. It was killing her.

She was jerked out of her heart's eruption as a loud blast from the church organ hit the first notes to the wedding march. She mindlessly stood up along with the rest of the congregation and would have buckled back onto the pew when Jesse suddenly stepped in to stand beside her if he hadn't grabbed her upper arm to steady her. She was shaking, but wasn't sure from what. Anger? Embarrassment? Delirious relief?

He didn't say a word, but pulled her down onto the seat beside him. Swallowing and swallowing, she couldn't stop the tears from springing in her eyes.

Jesse sat there looking down at her. She could feel his eyes on her, not to mention the hard warmth of his thigh pressed against her hip and leg. His arm rested on the back of the pew, his fingers scratching up and down on her arm. It was a comforting gesture. She knew he was trying to help her regain control, but the gentleness of this big, woodsy character was just making it worse. The coward! He could have told her! The rotten coward.

The wedding party had all entered and were in place up front when Jesse stood and took her hand, pulling her as quietly as possible beside him and out of the building. He stopped beside the jeep and suddenly pulled her against his chest. His arms wrapped her up and held her gently snug.

She let him hold her until she'd spent all the tears she had banked up. There had been so little of this kind of attention—gentle concern—in her life that she wanted to cling to him and beg him not to ever let her go. But she remembered that High Point Ranch was at stake and she didn't dare get suckered in by the man who had already joined her late husband in premeditated deceit against her. And hadn't he just now made a total fool of her?

The warmth of his arms suddenly became too agonizing and she easily pulled free and stepped away from him.

He abruptly opened the jeep door and waited for her to get in.

"Want something to eat?" he asked as he steered the all-terrain vehicle onto the highway. "There's a truck stop not far up ahead...Food's good." He shot a quick look at her tear stained face.

Fact was, she was starved. "I didn't bring my make-up bag."

He shot her an incredulous look. "Well, thats the best round about answer to the straightest question I've ever asked."

That was it. She couldn't hold it any longer. "Why didn't you tell me?" she blurted at him without blinking.

"You didn't ask."

"That's not what I mean and you know it."

"Then let me rephrase that. Fact is...you had a lesson to learn."

"Lesson to...Because I misunderstood yours and Bett's relationship...you felt you needed to...to humiliate me?"

"I felt I needed to teach you how to wait for facts before you let your mouth get you in trouble."

"But, you kissed me...and then let me believe you and Bett were..."

"Getting married? No. You assumed that without a viable reason...And then threatened me to boot. I told you, I don't take threats well."

Laura opened her mouth to throw back an argument, then quickly realized she didn't have one. She turned to look out her window, hating that he was right, but not forgetting for a split second that he was not a trustworthy friend.

By the time they were seated in the noisy café, Laura's appetite was gone. When she ordered only a cup of hot lemon tea, she refused to meet the pale gray eyes that shot her a quick glance.

Neither spoke from the time they sat down until Jesse pushed his empty plate aside and started on his freshly refilled coffee.

Jesse suddenly drew a long breath and reached across the table to lightly cover Laura's hand. She didn't know if she literally jumped at this unexpected move or just her insides flipped over. But she looked across the table and her gaze locked on his. The way he was looking at her was startling. She couldn't even blink.

Little did she know, Jesse was fighting an overwhelming attack of emotions. Not anything he was accustomed to. He had a strange feeling that there was far more to Laura Parker's presence in his life than he could put his finger on. But it wasn't all that sudden. Something had been niggling at him from the day he'd heard her voice making reservations for her and Andy.

Oh, there was the business with Matthew years ago. Laura had stood solidly between his and Matt's lifelong plans to jointly own and work a dude ranch together. The two had spent lots of time as kids working at and playing cowboy on a neighboring ranch, dreaming and planning right up through high school. And there was the property that Matt had insisted on buying anyway.

But there was something else. Entirely something else going on inside him that he couldn't shake. He searched his mind for a way to express himself now, if he could just come up with an opening.

Laura pulled her hand out from under his feathery, warm touch, but their eyes remained locked on each other.

Finally, "Laura...I'm sorry." He looked down at his still steaming coffee, then back up to her face. "I never meant to humiliate you. I realize now that's what I did tonight." Despite the fact that he knew he hadn't forgiven her for tearing his and Matt Parker's dreams apart, nor did he trust her reason for suddenly vacationing in a *barnyard*, as she had so aptly put it, there was still something floating around in the shadows of his brain. He hated that feeling. And yet his apology was heartfelt.

She tore her gaze away from him then. Unable to trust her voice, she simply nodded. Something was different about him suddenly. There was a gentle side to this cowboy that she'd have never believed if she wasn't seeing it and hearing it.

"There's something else I wanted to talk to you about...but not here. Let's get out of this noise." He couldn't believe he was going to discuss what he was going to discuss with her. He was compelled to say it. Almost *pushed* inside his gut.

Laura waited in the jeep while he paid the bill. She used the few minutes to collect herself. Here it comes, she thought. He was going to address High Point Ranch. Offer her a settlement. Hopefully he would be fair, then she and Andy could soon get back to their own lives. In Texas. That last thought brought a sudden heaviness in her heart.

Darkness had fallen and it seemed Jesse was deliberately driving slow. Laura stared at the dark road in front of her for a mile or so, then Jesse turned onto an even darker gravel road. Another half mile, he turned again and crossed a cattle guard to follow a jeep trail through an open rolling pasture. Any other day, she would have been frantically searching around for a weapon about now. But strangely, a peacefulness enveloped her entire being. It felt so oddly sweet, she just went with it.

Jesse stopped atop a big hill and turned off the engine. She followed his gaze straight up into a blue black night sky with millions of tiny silver twinkle lights.

"Beautiful...isn't it?" The deep coarseness of his voice caused Laura to look at him, then back up again. That deep gravel voice had grabbed and twisted her gut, way down deep until she put her hand on her stomach to hold everything in place.

She couldn't seem to get much above a whisper. "I don't remember ever noticing the stars like this...So many...It's hypnotizing." Impulsively, she turned toward Jesse and found him looking at her, his dark eyes questioning.

"Laura...Do you believe in God?"

The air around her shut off. She stared at him for a long time, stunned at what he had just asked her.

Frankly, Jesse couldn't believe how this was going either. Not in his thirty-eight years did he ever talk to anybody about God. Except to Donny. Once. That was back a few years ago when the younger Brandon had taken him to a Cowboy Church gathering hosted by the Double OO, a neighboring ranch owned by his now, good friends, Judd and Toni Luke.

Judd Luke had preached that night, a night Jesse would never forget for the rest of his days on earth, or thereafter. He had always believed God existed, but that night, he met Him, the Lord Jesus Christ, face to Face. It wasn't like anything he knew how to describe. But nothing looked, felt, smelled or tasted the same after that night that he had told Jesus he was sorry for his sins, then gave his life to Him. The same type of compelling he was feeling tonight had caused him to fall on his knees in a deep sorrowful repentance in the middle of the Luke's living room floor. He had laughed and cried together with Donny for hours after they left the Double OO. And that was the night that little brother Donny had told him that he believed God was calling him to preach.

Then life just resumed it's normal daily routine at High Point. Nothing else was changed over the years since. And Jesse had kept his spiritual business between himself and Jesus. Until tonight.

The unexpected question rocked her thought processes for a moment. She stared at him for a long minute trying to switch gears in her head.

Finally, she said, "God? You mean...do I think Matt and...and Dodger the horse are ranching together up in the sky...in a place called Heaven? No."

He studied her for an instant, really wanting to let this alone. But there was that thing going on inside of him that wouldn't let up.

"Sounds like we've both been talking to the same little boy." He smiled and gave her a sideways glance.

"Is that what you told him...about going to live in Heaven after you die?"

"Something close to that."

"Do you believe that pie-in-the-sky stuff?" she asked almost flippantly.

He hesitated a moment, but only because he suddenly felt the need to go slow with his answers to her. He also wished this night was over with. He was a fish out of water here, floundering around for words to a conversation he didn't want to have. This woman's spiritual life was her own business. He couldn't believe he had started the whole thing.

He heard himself say, "I believe there is a God. I believe He lives in Heaven," he pointed upward, "way up above those stars there."

"Why?" she asked, glaring.

"Why do I believe that?"

She glared harder without flickering an eyelash.

Jesse felt like his brain had suddenly lost a vital connection that he needed in order to continue this exchange. Whatever had compelled him into this God talk in the first place seemed to have hit a light's out switch.

Feeling a little dispirited, he turned fully toward her, draping an arm across the steering wheel, the other along the top of his seat back and looked at her. After a full half minute, he spoke slowly, thinking ahead of his words.

"Laura...I know plumb to my bone marrow that God is real. That...Heaven is a real place." He paused several seconds. "I believe this, but honestly...I don't know *why* I believe it."

The angry steam had gone out of her face and she closed her eyes and let her head fall back against her seat. The tenderness laced around his gruff voiced honesty almost had her in tears. They were both quiet for a long time.

Jesse studied her. Every contour and angle of her face, her wind-blown blonde layers all tousled and thinking he'd never seen a truly sexy woman before this moment. He looked away, telling himself not to go there, then, went there. Their gazes collided then and when she turned her face toward him slightly, he leaned over and pressed his mouth to hers.

So soft, those lips that pressed into his, returning the kiss and pushing for more. It had been a very long time since he'd had a woman so close to being in his arms. And right now his heart felt like a train engine at full throttle. And it scared him.

He had known a sweet unbridled passion for a woman once. He knew the intensity of love that makes an idiot out of a man. And he also knew the soul killing pain of losing that love. That memory felt like a splash of ice water in his face and he determined all over again to remember the cost of loving a woman. He had learned the lesson well, that nothing in this life is a surety of *happily ever after,* no matter how it starts off. He had become so embittered, his life consumed with resentment after Kate's betrayal only a week before their wedding. The one woman he thought he couldn't survive without. But he did survive. And he overcame the pure ugliness of waking up every morning knowing she wasn't there. He gave all that credit to the transforming power of Jesus Christ in his soul. He hadn't thought of Kate in years now, but neither had he allowed his heart's door to be cracked open to even hope for another chance at love. And this woman he was kissing, who was kissing him, who was roiling his senses into a category five hurricane, was only a woman like any other. But he had rejected many opportunities like this one over the years. Scores of young flirty *dudetts* had batted more than one eyelash his way while he distanced himself without much more than a nod of acknowledgment. So how had he managed to get himself into this moment?

Without warning, he pulled himself loose from her. He gazed down into her startled searching eyes for a long moment before slowly turning back around behind the steering wheel. For the first time since Kate, Jesse wanted the touch of a woman, felt a desire for female companionship. But not just any woman. This one. This one, God help him, who didn't believe in their Almighty Creator.

Laura recovered enough from the abrupt mood swing to study the man who didn't seem to have a clue what he had just done to her. She felt moved in a way she had never experienced before. Ever. The pleasure Jesse evoked inside her entire body by the mere touch of his hand was astonishing. But his kiss. Matthew had never made her feel like this. In fact, he had rarely ever kissed her. Not more than a quick peck on the mouth, even when they had made love. But this mountain of a man made her heart thump hard and her nerves ping pong until she had to grab her stomach to get control of the quivering. She had only known him for a few days and the fact was, she didn't know him at all. This primitive desire pounding in her bloodstream probably has a name. And one she might not want to know. One she shouldn't be having. Regardless, it hurt when he pulled away from her just now.

Before starting the jeep engine, Jesse paused for one more long look across the wide expanse of the moonlit valley in front of him. He needed a moment to get control of himself and he needed to know. So he asked.

"Tell me, Laura. What do you think of this place...High Point Ranch?"

Laura's back straightened, causing him to glance over at her. The warm passion he had just felt and seen on her the past few moments was suddenly stone cold.

Her throat tightened, thoughts racing from pain to anger. He had baited her. He had brought her out here and made a fool of her to find out what she knew.

With only a half top on the jeep, she felt the chilly night air for the first time breeze her face. She was parked out in the middle of nowhere with a man she barely knew and who probably hadn't said a total of five dozen words to her. One who fueled anger and resentment every time he did open his mouth. And now, one who raised her sexuality and longing straight up from the dead. And, for him, it was all a game. A sickening wave of self-reproach engulfed her, angering her even more that she was allowing herself to feel ashamed. That part of her sheltered past was changing right now, she promised herself.

With tilted chin, she looked him square in the eyes and barked, "I like this ranch just fine...Jesse."

His eyes widened on her. "That's good. Why am I not convinced?"

If that's the way he wanted to play—fine!

"Well...I guess I'll have to make a point to convince you."

He looked surprised at that and if she didn't know better, she'd have bought the confusion that darted through those gorgeous silver pools that washed her face.

The short drive back was silent and strained.

***

CHAPTER FIVE

Laura stalked out of the cabin before dawn, still rankled with a thousand conflicting emotions. These unfamiliar feelings were tearing her apart, keeping her awake most of the night. The strength of her sensuality had shocked her and obviously given Jesse a bad impression of her. A wrong impression.

It was a cold morning. A late season biting north wind was blowing, but she needed to feel the wind on her face. She absorbed the smells of the early morning walk through the grass and pine trees. After only a few minutes, the sweet smells of nature had strangely eased her overworked mind.

As much as she had thought it impossible, she was actually learning to love this place. The atmosphere was filled with solitude that she found herself yearning to be a part of. The high trees arched over head, the bright three quarter moon filtered down between their leaves and branches. Here, time passed so serenely you could easily lose track of it. There was no worry, no hustle, or bustle. Just time and peace—a strong soothing potion for whatever it was that ailed you.

Dawn was pinking through when she got back to the yard and noticed a stream of light that filtered under the barn door. Curiously she approached the door that was slightly cracked open, then entered at the sound of low murmuring that she couldn't make out. A familiar voice, speaking as if to a child, came from the expectant mare's stall. She peeked her head around where she could see through the length of the extra large, roomy pen and found Cook on his knees and bent over the downed chestnut. He was stroking her neck as she made noises of her own as though answering him.

Sensing his audience, Cook turned his head to look at Laura, then rose to his feet, removing his hat spontaneously.

"Miz Parker, you're up early this morning."

Suddenly the mare gave an agonizing cry, lifted her head up, then lay back flat on the ground.

"Is she going to be all right, Mr. Walton?"

"Well, I'm figurin she will be. I might need to help her a little...Have to wait and see."

"Should I go get Jesse or Donny to help you?"

"They left the ranch hours ago and I don't think she'll wait much longer. I have a call in for a boy who does our veterinary work if I need it. Works over to the Double OO."

She wondered where the two Brandon's had gone, but the little mare's cries blotted out the thought as fast as it had come.

"What can I do, Hank?"

"Aw, Mam..."

What was it with these cowboys and *mam*? "Hank, I don't know anything about birthing a baby horse...but I'm all you have right now. It's my guess that mama would be grateful to whoever helped her through this."

Hank looked away from her toward the mare. When he looked at her again, Laura was sure the lines in his face had relaxed.

He tossed his tattered old straw hat to the ground and motioned toward the opposite side of the barn. "Fetch me a towel out of that barrel over there and let's see what we can do for Miss Bella."

She grabbed the towel, then eased into the pen and dropped to her knees beside Hank.

"What kind of trouble is she having, Hank?"

"Don't rightly know. Hopefully none. She paced around this stall for two...three hours, then she laid down. Usually the colt comes within fifteen or twenty minutes after that and it's been forty-five. Can't let her wait too long."

A contraction rolled through Miss Bella then and brought a huge gush of bloody water. Within seconds, two tiny hoofs protruded, then a nose.

"Oh lordy...it's comin real fast." His voice was only a whisper, but was laced with excitement.

The tiny head popped through only a couple seconds before the rest of it's body slid out onto a soft bed of fresh hay. The birth sack was plastered over the baby's face and nose.

"Laura, hurry up and pull that sack off it's face." Hank instructed her on what to do, but didn't make a move to help her. The sound of her first name spoken by the older gentleman gave her a feeling of unity with this event.

She grabbed the slimy membrane and pulled the baby free of it.

-336 "Now...take your towel and rub her face and body with it. Get her breathing fired up good." Hank spoke quietly and calmly.

Her! "It's a girl?"

He nodded, the smile on his lips reaching into the squint in his eyes.

Afterwards, Laura put her arms around the silky wetness of the foal's neck, smelling it's newborn warmth.

"I couldn't have done it better myself," came a new voice from behind the pair of contented *midwives.*

"Hello, Les." Hank stood and offered his hand to the neighboring veterinarian.

Laura retreated as well when the mare rose up to examine her new offspring.

"Les, this is Laura Parker. She and her boy are guests of the ranch."

"Les Kane...mam." He shook her hand, his brown eyes friendly and sleepy. Then he immediately took charge of the patients to complete their care.

Laura watched him a few moments. She decided *mam* was just going to have to be tolerated. She also decided it must be true. All cowboys *were* good looking!

Satisfied with a job well done, Hank left to fire up the camp breakfast. Laura exited the barn basking in a warm glow of pride. It seemed as though she had won something in there. Not like a competition trophy, but something very meaningful. A fulfillment in her soul.

Back inside her cabin, she showered and dressed for work. Andy was up and headed for the chuck wagon before she had time to tell him the news about the new baby. However, she discovered a short while later as she made her way toward the chuck wagon that Hank had already sang her praises to all the dudes.

She couldn't stop herself from feeling a little important after all the words of praise. Donny was back from wherever, patting her back and giving her praise through a mouth full of scrambled eggs.

Jesse still seemed to be missing and she had to clamp her teeth together to keep from asking Donny where he went. Before her curiosity could take control, she walked to the office, not really enthused with the prospect of being cooped up inside today. A hand scribbled note had been left for her on the desk. Jesse would be gone all day and would she *hold the fort* until his return. *Run the place like your own,* he'd written. She smiled. Why shouldn't she?

She sat down behind the desk and pulled out the paper file of documents again. This would be a perfect time to read the contents closely.

"Oh!" Her mouth went dry and she froze in shock at finding the papers gone. She dug around in the file drawer, hoping they had just been put in another place. They weren't there. Jesse must have taken the file. She had no idea what he was up to, but felt sure he was expending some effort to prevent her from being legally able to stake a claim on this ranch. But, her lawyer had the information. He had told her as much. What could Jesse possibly do?

Before she could think further, Donny stepped through the open doorway of the office.

"How's it going, Laura? Thought I'd check to see if you needed anything before I take a group on a trail ride."

"It's been a slow morning. The phone hasn't rung once."

He glanced around the office and ginned. "Like what you did in here. It's amazing what a little know-how can do to a place."

"Thanks."

"So what's the schedule looking like?"

"Actually...I've given out a lot of information on the phone... but so far only two couples have booked."

He pulled his face into a tight grimace and bugged his eyes out for extra emphasis.

She knew he was trying to be funny, but wondered if there was a true down side to there not being many customers scheduled.

"Not too good, I guess?" she queried him.

He started to turn away, then stopped at her question and took off his bent up black Stetson. A light plume of dust swirled in the air when he popped it once against his leg.

"Oh, sorry. Guess I should do that outside."

She couldn't help but grin at the sweetness of this kid. What a catch for a lucky young lady someday.

He walked over closer to the desk where she sat. "Actually, Mrs...uh, Laura...High Point is not doing real good right now. We just don't seem to attract as many people here as some other dude ranches around the area. Jesse has talked about shutting down and I hate to think what that would do to him."

She was stunned at the news. "I'm sorry to hear this."

"Yeah...me too. I've been praying to the Lord everyday about what to do. I know God has a plan...He'll bring it around. Right now, I better get to trail bossin' before Andy does it for me." He settled his hat back on his head, grinned and winked at Laura, then stalked out.

She stared at the doorway in disbelief. What was all this *God* talk? Did Donny really believe there was somebody like a God who was going to help this little speck-of-dust ranch on this big earth? Jesse believed in God, but didn't have a clue *why* he did. So what's up with that? Had somebody brainwashed these two men?

So, God's the Man with the plan, huh? What next!

Suddenly and slowly, an idea moved through her mind, almost making her laugh out loud. This idea sounded crazy. Impossible, actually. What did she know about ranch life? She had barely stuck her head outdoors in the city where she lived. She realized she was trembling and it was partly with excitement at this nutty idea. The other part was that she had no clue whatsoever how a person would begin such an undertaking. And why she would even consider such a thing went way past her intellect. Or past the cutoff button before you get to stupid. She wasn't a go-getter business brain. And why was she sitting here arguing with herself. Fresh oxygen! Her brain cells must be starving for air.

Laura left headquarters sensing an unusual lightness in her steps. She headed for the barn where the trail riders were dismounting and moaning at their stiff muscles.

Immediately, she imagined a huge hot tub steaming beneath a lodge pole arbor, inviting those aching backsides to take a soaking plunge. *Wouldn't these dudes love that about now!*

That image excited her beyond reason and at the same time, she knew the only logical and safe answer to this madness that was overtaking her mind was to load up her son and suitcases and go home and forget High Point Dude Ranch existed.

Instead, she did the next best thing. She found Andy and decided to spend the rest of the day doing whatever five year olds do at a dude ranch.

Through pure determined grit, she made the day clinging awkwardly to leather and horse hair while Andy instructed her on how to ride. He had progressed so well, Jesse now allowed him to ride around a safe perimeter of the ranch yard. He had insisted she spend the day trotting and loping inside the corral so she could ride outside with him next time.

By late afternoon, she barely managed to drag herself to the chow line while that imaginary hot tub imprinted a visual of itself in her head, front and center.

The pair retired to their cabin early. It took all of ten minutes for Andy to be bathed and sound asleep.

0   Laura followed suit, except for the sound asleep part. By midnight, she turned up the flame in the fireplace and settled herself in front of it with a mug of decaf coffee.

She couldn't shake off the hair-brained idea of using her and Andy's *money to live on* to update this ranch. Where was this coming from? It's not like she was a frivolous risk taker.

Unreasonably, she took a blaming potshot at Matthew Parker for this ridiculous mess. He had bought this place behind her back, obviously hoping she would change her mind.

Matt was a private person and he had gone to great lengths to shelter her and Andy from the rest of the world. But now, she wondered about the love he'd so adamantly demanded that she accept from him. He had more than suggested that his way for her as his wife and as Andy's mother was the only correct way. He seemed to know best about every issue and her rare attempts to express her own ideas were immediately opposed.

And she had accepted his *fatherly* devotion. That's all she knew. She never knew a dad. Never had a male in her life until Matthew Parker. She had loved him the way he had taught her to. She had never once thought that something was missing from her relationship with her husband. He was always right there, taking care of her every need. But he'd never wrapped her up in his arms and held her. *Really* held her. He had never kissed her like, like

And speaking of Jesse Brandon!

The next potshot was all his! He was obviously a liar, a schemer and a thief. But he had awakened something on the inside of her that she never knew was there. A different kind of emotion between a man and a woman. He had kissed her, held her, bared his soul to her about his belief in a God who lived in Heaven and then, he took off with some kind of papers that said her deceased husband was part owner of High Point. And to do what?

Her ramblings were cut off suddenly by that same image of a bubbling hot tub nestled beneath a log arbor. Out of nowhere, the mental picture popped into her mind and created a fresh wave of excitement. The provocation seemed to take on it's on life inside of her. She was stunned. She was mesmerized. Was she nuts?

Well, Jesse did tell her to run the place like her own. And she had that in writing! Besides, it *was* her own. That was already an established fact as far as she was concerned.

She closed her eyes and sucked a deep, slow breath. She knew she was about to launch feet first into Dude Ranching 101.

The instant that Laura's feet hit the floor the next morning, she howled out loud. It felt like someone had just hit her in the crotch with a grenade. Oh geez, if this is what riding a horse does to you, she'd rather be boiled in oil!

Andy was already gone, of course. Donny had asked last evening for his help as an honorary sidekick for the day.

After soaking as much as a body can soak in a hot shower and downing half a pot of coffee, she filled a paper plate with cheese and crackers and crippled into headquarters.

She hadn't seen a soul this morning. Come to think of it, she had noticed only a small handful of the usual group were under the pavilion for breakfast. After checking the schedule, she realized most had already spent their week and had gone home. She had not seen Jesse since day before yesterday. If he didn't appear soon, she would bite the bullet and ask Donny where he had gone.

By noon, Laura had learned that Jesse Brandon had not moved this ranch too far out of the Stone Age as far as utilizing the Internet for business or creating a few extra incentives for different age and social groups. Like a cabin/honeymoon suite, for instance. She barely suppressed a squeal as her decorating gift kicked in with ideas for that one cabin.

Her mind was popping out ideas so fast she didn't know what to do with them. She felt overwhelmed, yet this whole thing was burning like an out of control fire in her middle as she paced back and forth across the office, her brain clicking away.

This would take more people to operate it, more buildings, more animals and money. The financial part stopped her for only a moment. If Jesse was considering closing up shop, then he probably didn't have money lying around for all that. But she did. At least she could get the ball rolling. Once business picked up, the rest would work itself out. Right?

She should present all of this to Jesse as soon as he was back from trying to screw her over. Even though she would really rather not. But there was no way to do all this and hide it. Was there? Nah.

Jesse sat alone in his motel room, socked feet propped in the chair across from the one he occupied. Oklahoma was too hot for him. But the deed was accomplished and in the morning he'd be out of here. Out of here and back home to Wyoming so he could get this ordeal dealt with finally.

Lawyer Baines hadn't been much help to him in making this decision. Laura Parker had blind sided him, showing up out of the blue like that. And even though his emotions were, *without his consent*, all tangled up in his boyhood friend's widow and son, he felt like a traitor to Matthew. But, as much as he had loved his friend, he could see how he might have helped him deceive Laura.

0   Anger had roared through him every time he thought of Matt's self-centered wife. She had shut down even a simple conversation with Matthew when he'd desperately wanted to experience his lifelong dream of *cowboying up north*. The two wanna-be wranglers had planned it all. Then as life goes, they pursued other interest for a few years.

Jesse had been the first to wander back to the original plan and then present it to his surprised friend on a visit through their home town where Matt had settled with his family.

In the end, Matthew decided to do the next best thing and bought two hundred acres that adjoined High Point Dude Ranch. Jesse had agreed to take the title deed in his own name, in the event Matt wasn't around to see it through, and see that it was signed over to Andy when he reached legal age. Who would have guessed?

The trust Matt had placed in him was major. And never would he have betrayed that trust. But he was positive that Laura knew about this land deed now, and *something* that he believed in his heart was a divine leading, was urging him to clean up this deceitful act. So he did that today. At least, legally.

He had already learned that getting into agreement with God quickly made circumstances work out better. At least, it seemed that way. But then again, some issues *HE* doesn't seem to care much about. Jesse was losing his ranch and his faith for God to help him out was not holding up too good either.

There wasn't enough time to make it now, even if the ranch filled up tomorrow with dudes. This last group got his help paid and the lights burning one more month. And to top it all off, he was scared that his heart was in for another rough ride. He wondered what Matt would think if he knew how much his trusted old friend wanted his widowed wife and his young son for himself. The fact that she didn't believe in Almighty God didn't defuse that wanting one bit. And that bothered him.

He was going home with the documents to sign over the neighboring property to Laura, praying she would do right by Andy in due time.

But first, he had to hold over an extra day to visit an old family friend.

Three phone inquiries and no new customers was all Laura had to show for business all day. Except for her detailed, inartistic drawing of her brand new and improved version of High Point Dude Ranch.

She took a copy of the original brochure and added a list of simple activities just for kids. Besides the established hay ride and horseback rides, she added feeding and grooming instruction, a sectioned off swimming hole in the creek, storytelling around a campfire, with smores, of course, camp out in an Indian village, complete with teepees and a petting zoo. Then, with a semi load of hay bales.

Her creative rambling screeched to a halt when the front screen door squeaked open, then shut after a noisy entrance by someone. Andy, she figured, until a salt and pepper gray head peeped around the door at her. The long, narrow face was age wrinkled with a set of smiling blue eyes that twinkled in genuine sweetness.

"Hi," she chirped. "I know you're Laura...I'm Martha. The boys already told me all about you and the little boy."

It took a couple seconds, then she remembered Donny had mentioned Martha, the cleaning lady.

"Hi." She finally answered while she watched the lady's eyes dart around the rearranged office, still twinkling, then settle back on Laura.

"Nice work. Did you doll up this *man-cave* in here?"

Laura smiled broadly and nodded, really liking this Martha.

"I'll put my stuff in my room and make us coffee." She reached behind her and picked up an overstuffed medium sized bag. "Come on out to the kitchen...Ten minutes."

Martha walked past the open office door and disappeared down the hall. She reminded Laura of a string bean. Tall and 0thin with a little wiry mixed in. She guessed her to be around fifty.

After one long phone call explaining all the new soon coming events at High Point to a potential future customer, Laura found her way to the kitchen, wondering how Martha knew she was a coffee drinker.

The kitchen was unexpectedly huge and well furnished, but emptiness resonated throughout the room. Only the wonderful aroma of fresh dripped coffee was inviting enough to touch it with warmth.

An extra wide and long butcher block island covered the middle of the floor. A wagon wheel style rack that held all shapes and sizes of pots and pans hung from the ceiling, centered above the island. The coffee maker, two big mugs, cream, sugar and Martha occupied a spot beneath the cookware.

"Grab that stool, honey." She gestured at a spot across the counter from her. "What a treat this is!" She filled both mugs. "I don't get much female company in here for coffee. Betsy wasn't here that much and didn't slow down for a chit chat break when she was. When Donny told me I had a coffee drinking buddy in here...I hugged him."

Both women laughed out loud, while a friendship bonded over the next hour.

"So...how often do you come here, Martha?"

"Oh, couple times a week usually. But I'm here to stay until Jesse gets back and things get back to normal. Maybe only a night...Maybe two. Don't matter to me. I live alone...Rent an apartment in Jackson. I've done these two boys laundry and dusting for, oh, guess about three...four years now. They gave me my own room and said I could stay out here all I wanted...but I won't take advantage. Hank cooks all the meals outside so the kitchen never gets much use."

Laura thought she may have caught an extra twinkle in Martha's right eye when she spoke Hank's name. In fact, she was sure of it.

"And the best part is...I get to help look after your little Andy if things get too busy around here."

Laura's mind wandered suddenly to Jesse, wondering if she should ask if Martha knew where he went and why. Had either of the Brandon brothers confided in this woman over the years? About this property or about Matthew?

"If that's okay by you, that is."

She jerked back into the moment and realized Martha's face had turned solemn .

"What?" Laura was embarrassed. Too much working her brain at once. Finally the woman's words caught up to her mind. "Oh...it's more than okay. We'll make you his honorary Grandmother. He's never known a grandparent in his life."

"That would be wonderful." The older woman's smile returned, then she focused a more serious squint on her coffee klatch guest. "You can talk to me if you want to, Laura. I chatter like a magpie, but not about important things...I just listen to those." Martha filled up both cups again, then leaned forward, resting her forearms on the counter top and waited.

Laura really wanted to spill herself to somebody, but not to a stranger she knew little about. But again, what the heck.

Martha's eyes widened, pushing her to get started.

Laura bit at her bottom lip. "Do you know where Jesse went?"

"No. Do you?"

For the next half hour, Laura poured out her story, finishing up with a simple outline of her ideas to help get the ranch back in many vacationer's plans around the country.

"Lord a mercy." Martha sat up straighter on her stool. "This would make a great soap opera...except this isn't make believe. I knew the ranch wasn't doing too well. Hank told me he thought it was in trouble."

"I'm not a business woman, Martha. I don't know anything about financial dealings. But I have this sense of what families would enjoy at a place like this." She gazed into Martha's stunned stare. "And I have the money to get it started. I just don't know exactly what to do first."

"But...you don't really have proof that you share ownership of this place."

"I'm sure enough of it. I know what Matt and Jesse's plans were and I saw the paperwork with Matthew's name. I think it said two hundred acres. And now the papers are missing and Jesse has disappeared. I don't know where he went or for how long or why he took that information...but I do know that he helped my husband lie to me. And if I decide to push my weight around this…this…" she waved her arm through the air, not conscious of the anger she was displaying, "big… barely-making-it mound of manure…this…this…beautiful… peaceful…soul jarring piece of earth…then I have every right! And as far as I'm concerned…it's long overdue."

"Oh, my!" Martha's blue eyes were huge and the twinkles in them were jitterbugging. She had prayed so hard for a way to help *her men* save this little enterprise. The answer had arrived.

She picked up her nearly empty coffee cup and held it out toward Laura. "I got nothing better to do, girlfriend. Let's go for it!"

Tears welled in Laura's eyes, mainly because the excitement inside of her was at explosion level and she knew she was doing a good thing, even if a twinge of revenge was edged around her emotions.

Instinctively, she grabbed up her half full cup of cold Java and clinked it against the one waiting for her. At that same instant, strange words floated quietly through her mind: *ALL THINGS WORK TOGETHER.* That toast she took of the creamy, stale liquid was the best drink of coffee she had ever tasted!

Jesse opened his eyes trying to judge where that unnerving buzz was coming from. Then he remembered and reached over to flick off the ancient alarm clock. He stretched as far as his fingers and toes would let him, then sat up and pulled on jeans, boots and the one T-shirt he'd brought.

He couldn't believe he'd let himself get wrangled into this one, but he guessed somebody had to do it.

Lex Farmer had sent a letter a few weeks back asking for Jesse to come visit him real soon. And to his shame, he had actually forgotten about it until he had to make this little business trip through Oklahoma anyway.

He opened the bunkhouse door and let his eyes slowly roam around the old ranch that was his and Matthew Parker's home away from home when they were kids. This was where the *cowboying* bug had bit both of them. Nights spent in this same bunkhouse is where their dreams and plans were made to own a ranch someday.

Mr. Lex had let them ride his horses and rope at his cows and laughed long and loud when one or the other of them ended up on his butt in the dirt. And that was most of the time.

Jesse pulled the creaky door shut behind him and walked out into the breaking dawn. He had insisted on sleeping out here, not realizing how deep in dirt the old building was. But an armload of clean linens and a few dozen swipes down the walls and across the floor with a broom got him through.

He really didn't want to be here. He had plenty to do at his own ranch, but Donny had assured him the crowd had thinned with nothing else on the horizon in the way of new dudes signed up.

His eyes scanned the perimeter of the ranch. Just like his dreams of a thriving dude ranch, this place was literally falling apart. The roof on the old house needed some serious patching, but the hay barn was the old man's main complaint.

Mr. Lex was almost ninety and bedridden. His live-in care givers were a man and wife team nearly as old as he was and not able to keep up with much more than caring for him around the clock.

The stubborn old coot wouldn't give it up. He still had a few head of *old* cows, one *old* horse and a load of hay in a barn that was almost minus a roof. And somehow, Jesse had managed to get himself talked into doing a *few chores* around here before he left.

He sucked his lungs full of clean air and exhaled slowly. Looking around, remembering the best years of his boyhood, he realized this place was part of his legacy—his passion for living the life of a cowboy, his riding ability, his love for working and living ranch life, was all given to him by Mr. Lex.

Jesse's dad hadn't been around much when he and his brother were growing up. At some point, he'd found another woman and kids he liked better and he disappeared. Jesse had been the closest thing to a dad Donny ever knew.

Their mom had suffered a stroke and died the same day when Donny was around thirteen. Jesse had taken him to Wyoming to live and go to school and the brothers had worked High Point Dude Ranch until this very day. Five freaking years of struggling just to stay afloat and now the ranch was going to fold anyway.

He thought of Laura. And for the hundredth time in days, he pushed the thought of her away. What did he have to offer a woman? Or a little boy? At least her dead husband had provided something, even if he had to be deceitful about it. Knowing Matthew, he would have well provided for his family. Jesse gritted his teeth until he felt a painful pressure. He realized then he was letting his thoughts set him up for a really *bad* day.

He turned and glanced just to his left. Lights were on in the house. He'd been invited, no, commanded to have coffee and breakfast with the Diamonds. They made sure to ask what time he would be up and sure enough, he could smell the bacon frying. The name *Diamond* certainly fit this pair.

A couple hours later, Jesse sat on top of the barn roof, what there was of it, armed with scavenged sheets of galvanized tin and roofing nails and grumbled like he'd received an unjust sentence to a rock pile.

At that moment, the front door of the house banged shut. He turned his head and watched Mr. and Mrs. Diamond fuss over Lex as they worked together to angle his half laid back wheel chair where he could see Jesse on top of the barn.

He had sat beside Lex's bed yesterday and listened while the old man had reminisced about Jesse's and Matt's shenanigans back in the day. Jesse was surprised at the details the he had recalled and how slick he had cornered him into at least a week's worth of hard labor, if he worked fast!

He watched as Mr. Diamond gently worked a pair of eye glasses onto Lex's face, then pointed up at Jesse.

Lex was looking up at him and Jesse raised his hand that held a hammer. A yearning plea creased around the old man's eyes and Jesse's heart fell into his boots. That gentleman's life was over. He couldn't hammer tin onto his roof or stretch new wire on his broken down fences or throw a little hay to his livestock. He couldn't even get a cup of coffee for himself. He suddenly felt like a jerk for belly aching and moaning.

He ducked his head and swallowed hard. *Forgive me, Lord. There's no bigger ass on this earth than me today.* He didn't know if he could say *ass* when talking to God, but he couldn't think of a completely clean word to describe himself at the moment.

He glanced back at those ripened, red-rimmed eyes that were still fixed on him and silently promised God and Mr. Lex that he'd do his best to help out here for a few days and be thankful he could.

The next two weeks blurred by for Laura. Donny had told her and her new sidekick, Martha, that Jesse was helping out an old friend for a few days.

Laura and Martha had told Donny they were on a secret mission and convinced him not to spoil it for them.

Thus ensued some fast work. One trip into Jackson arranged for a brand new hot tub, fully installed immediately. A landscaping company contracted to handle the ground work under and around the new installation. New patio tables, chairs and loungers were loaded into Martha's old pickup and within two days, one gorgeous hot tub sat amid all sizes of clay pots filled with trees, flowers and cacti. The sitting and lounge area was more beautiful than either one of it's creators had imagined it. A small portable bathhouse was added to hold maintenance supplies and towels with room for winter storage.

About an acre away, behind the pavilion, pickups had emerged carrying supplies to erect four full size Indian teepees. They would be set in a large circle, all door flaps facing each other. The two women scouted the area for perfect sized rocks to be placed in a circle for a campfire.

Miraculously, not one person had ventured to ask what was going on. Laura assumed Donny had taken care of that.

After conversing with Hank Walton on about the fifth morning of activity, Martha went in search of Laura, finding her sitting in the dirt beside her cabin and shooting a wild game of marbles with Andy. Laura had just won the match, hands down, then tasseled Andy's hair, that had grown entirely too long.

"You let me win, didn't you, young man?" she teased.

"Aw, Mom, if I didn't let you sometimes...you might quit playing with me."

She laughed out loud. "Yeah, I just might. You better keep on letting me win some."

"I will. I promise." He grinned broadly and she had to stop herself from grabbing him up in a bear hug. He only allowed that behind closed door these days.

Laura got up and walked to where Martha stood, arms folded and frowning.

"What's the matter?" she asked cautiously.

"Well, I...uh...just hired a couple of the ranch hands to put up some small animal pens for the petting zoo. You need to come show them what you want exactly."

Laura kept her eyes fixed on Martha's. "Okay. And while we're headed that way...you can tell me what's bothering you."

Without hesitation, Martha put it out there. "Hank asked me what this was all about. I hope you don't mind, but me and Hank...we go way back. We don't keep secrets from each other. I told him a little bit about your husband owning part of this place. He wouldn't tell me much, Laura, but said he was afraid you had gotten your facts tangled up a mite. Said he wouldn't be informing anybody about anything, but he did warn me that when Jesse got home...we two had best be hid out for a few hours until the *sawdust settled...*as he put it."

Laura was not in the least rattled by what Hank had said. And after a thoughtful silence, she said, "Martha, look around us. It's too late now to rethink anything. But, I don't think Jesse would have told anyone the truth about his and Matthew's dealings. He wasn't going to tell me. I happened on to the information...then he grabbed it and disappeared."

The two cohorts were quiet for a long minute as they both gazed around at the transformation of the immediate ranch yard. It was a beautiful setting and the teepees peeking up over the top of the newly decorated pavilion would thrill any kid and a few *grown up* kids as well.

Laura was surprised at the thrill she felt at the idea of a real Indian village campout with a group of young kids. Watching the village come to life stick by stone would have looked like foolishness a few short weeks ago. Now, it seemed magical. She suddenly felt like one of those grown up kids, herself.

The hot tub and *Garden of Eden* patio was something to behold. Both women feasted their eyes on that spot. It was romance personified out there in the middle of the old west scene.

Martha had been in love with Hank Walton for several years now, but coming from the old school, she had waited for him to make the first move. She knew he felt something for her. It was in those big brown eyes when he looked at her. He had even kissed her once when they were dancing. And right now, this newly created lovers paradise was conjuring up a mental image of the stubborn old cowpoke in the hot tub with her.

Laura, for the first time since Jesse had left, admitted to herself that she missed him terribly. This beautiful patio wouldn't even be that attractive to her, except for her image of Jesse sharing it with her. Not now, anyway. He may have lied and deceived her along with Matt. He may already have stolen all this from her. But she knew he had already moved himself into a place in her heart. She realized it wasn't this ranch that she wanted. She wanted Jesse. She wanted him to want her, to love her. She wanted the image of the two of them sharing that hot tub to become a reality.

Laura realized then that her motherly friend was staring at her and grinning. "I know a lovesick expression when I see one. Anybody I know?"

"That's nonsense, Martha. I was just wondering if Jesse might be really mad about all this. My rights are one thing, but it's going to be a shock when he first sees it. Hank might have a good point."

"Having self-doubts at this point is..."

"Oh, no. I'm not sorry about all this. I just..."

"Laura, you can stop trying to pitch this old lady a line. I've been around this block before. You're scared that you might have stepped over the line a little too far with Jesse and stand a good chance of getting your heart broke."

She looked into Laura's huge, round eyes that suddenly filled up. "Well, that's answer enough. Lord a mercy. This just gets better and better."

Laura couldn't keep from laughing through her sniffing. "For who?"

"I guess we'll find that out at the end of the road." She gestured toward a couple of cowboys standing down the drive. "Let's go get those guys started on the zoo project...then I want you to come with me. I want to show you something."

Laura turned to speak to Andy, but, of course, he was gone. In a second she spotted him doggin a step behind Donny and Hank who were headed toward the barn. Hank stopped abruptly and spoke to Andy as he pointed at Laura. At first, she was afraid he had worn out his welcome when Andy turned and ran to her.

"Mom, me and Mr. Brandon and Mr. Walton are going fishing. Mr. Walton said to ask your permission. But I can't catch a big one cause Mr. Brandon said if I catch the biggest fish again today...he was going to spank my butt." Andy giggled, his eyes as bright as a new penny.

Laura's eyes gathered tears of joy at her son's happiness. She knew she'd stick her neck out twice as far as she already had if it would bring this much joy that child.

"Go. Have fun...mind your manners...catch ten little bitty ones!"

"I will," he yelled into the space in front of him as he ran back to catch up.

With the ranch void of customers, Laura returned several phone messages asking for information, then jumped into the passenger side of Martha's truck.

0   "So. What did you want to show me, Miss Martha?"

"Hang on to your shirt tail...girlfriend. You're gonna love this."

Martha shot the old truck through an open gate behind the barn and onto a barely visible four-wheel vehicle path.

Laura had already decided that this country life, away from city noise, street lights, crowds of people, was something she could live with and truly love it. But Martha might be taking this good country life a little far into the backwoods for her taste.

The truck fairly flew down into a dry gully and straight back up the other side, then wound through a thickly wooded area before Martha finally pulled to a stop in front of—what? A potty stop at an antique outhouse?

Martha sat looking at that old shack like it was her own producing gold mine. "Here we are," she quipped excitedly.

Laura blinked. Then blinked again. Then she shot Martha a sideways omg look. "Uh, you go ahead...I don't have to go."

It took just a few seconds to catch her meaning before Martha slapped the steering wheel and roared with laughter. "G...Get...out."

They got out and met at the front of the truck. Martha bent at the middle holding her stomach. She was in uncontrolled hysterics. Finally, she managed to squeal, "This is our honeymoon suite!"

That did it. Laura glanced once more at the old shack and doubled over alongside her laughing sidekick. It was a long couple of minutes before the pair got control. The final sobering came for Laura when she realized that Martha was not joking.

"I don't know how much is left in your budget, but you did mention doing up a honeymoon cabin."

"Martha, there's not enough money in the state of Wyoming to turn this...*piece*...into an attraction for newlyweds. Tell me you're not serious!"

"As a heart attack." The look on Laura's face almost brought a case of giggles back to the older woman. "It's in better shape than you think. Let's look inside then we'll talk about it."

Laura trailed behind her friend up the surprisingly sturdy steps and onto a more surprising solid little porch. The rails around the small deck were even strong. The post and overhead awning appeared all together as well.

But, when she stepped inside the structure, she was even more amazed. A quick scan around the interior revealed a lot of dirt and cobwebs and other than that, it was the most charming little cabin Laura could have ever dreamed up. A set of bunk beds hugged the far wall. A crude, rock fireplace was cut into the wall beside the doorway.

On the other side was a small kitchen area complete with a small microwave? A sink with running water? A small refrigerator? An oblong cedar table with notched split log benches on either side of it finished off its rustic charm.

"How are these utilities available way out here?"

"That's the beauty of this, Laura. It's not as far out as it appears. But a rustic atmosphere is what you want...without lacking the most basic of necessities. There's a water well out back and electricity. This was an old line shack used back when, but it's been modernized just enough to be a comfortable little love nest...Look in here."

Martha opened a door on the back wall that Laura hadn't noticed. There was an empty room and a tiny, but full bathroom tucked in the corner.

"Oh, Martha. Any couple that would choose a dude ranch for a honeymoon would adore this place...after we work our kind of magic on it...of course."

***

CHAPTER SIX

Jesse couldn't believe his luck or the way his silly heart was triple-timing in his chest. When he'd called home last night to say he was on his way back, Donny told him that Laura had decided to stay another week or so.

There wasn't a dude on the place, but his brother had bragged on how Laura and Martha had spruced the place up a little. He grinned as he watched a few more white lines disappear underneath the front end of his Ford dually. He could envision all the furniture in the house, completely rearranged. Maybe the walls in the kitchen were bright yellow now instead of dingy off-white. He could live with that.

Then again, what difference would it make? He couldn't run a business with no customers. Five years ago, he'd envisioned a busy, thriving ranch full of horse riders and fishermen and an old chuck wagon for a kitchen. And for the most part, that's what he had. But dude ranching seemed to have caught on around the area, and High Point's old west fare couldn't compete with swimming pools and recreational halls, tennis courts and the like. To Jesse, that just didn't seem like a real *ranch* experience. But his pocketbook could never measure up to that anyway. Not nearly!

He'd done a lot of soul searching the past days, not at all sure he had found any answers. He wasn't sure he could face his own self in the mirror without feeling the shame of failure. He had six people on payroll that were about to be out of a job.

He hated what he was thinking, but couldn't seem to stop the surge of anger roiling in his mind. Where was God in all this defeat? It seemed to Jesse that his life had been one long struggle. His dad ran out on the family, his mom had worked herself into an early grave trying to go it alone with two little boys and his dude ranch venture, the heart and soul of his dreams, had fizzled. Nothing seemed to have changed much after his surrender to Jesus Christ, except his way of thinking and trying to do good by people.

His little brother had grown up to be a good Christian man. That should be enough satisfaction for him right there.

But it wasn't enough for him right this minute. He was angry. A good pity party was in progress in the front seat of his truck and he just felt due.

He didn't try to shut out the memory of Laura this time— the way she had fit so perfectly in his arms. He thought he'd been in love once, but now he didn't think so. This was a new depth of feeling he had for Laura Parker. Something brand new had slammed his heart solidly and literally against his ribcage when his lips touched hers. As if he didn't have enough failure to deal with. He figured this aching coldness that crept through his guts, knowing he didn't have one single thing to offer the woman he'd already lost his heart to, was going to be his undoing.

"And do YOU know what else?" He ranted out loud to God, figuring he was already one step inside of his Father's woodshed anyhow. "I couldn't even tell the lady *why* I believe you really exist!"

A hard lump suddenly formed in his throat. Despair was not something he was used to feeling, but it had taken hold on him and he hated it.

Lord, help me out here. Forgive my anger. I just don't know what to do.

He was only a few miles from High Point when it hit him. He wasn't headed home, but had detoured and was about to pull up in front of Judd and Toni Luke's big log home. Had he fallen asleep? Not hardly, yet he didn't recall deciding to come by the Double OO Ranch. Before he could circle around and leave, he saw Judd making his way across the front yard, his arm high and waving.

Jesse rolled his window down as Judd approached.

"Hello, neightbor." Judd reached in and slapped Jesse's shoulder. "Glad to see you're back. I heard you went south for a few days."

"Yeah, I haven't been home yet." Jesse felt ridiculously confused, then stupid when a hard knot closed his throat. He didn't know what he was doing here, but couldn't seem to excuse himself and drive on. He stared at his hands that were gripping the steering wheel and kept swallowing.

Without another word, Judd walked around the front of the dually, climbed in the passenger seat and shut the door.

The men sat in silence for a long while. Judd prayed silently, waiting, knowing Jesse hadn't shown up by accident.

Judd's thoughts raced back almost four years to the day that Toni Barton had shown up at his door expecting to work for him as a ranch hand. He didn't know it then, but that little bombshell of a cowgirl was sent Special Delivery to his front door and was used as a lariat by Almighty God to rope and drag his backslidden soul back to the right trail. And somewhere in the process, he'd fallen head first up to his toes in love with her. And bless God, she fell in, toes up, with him.

In short order, they wed and Toni soon gave him the most precious gift of his life—their little daughter, Abigail, now three years old. Before Abby was six months old, Judd became aware that God had something special for him to do. A fire began to build up in his bones to preach the Word of God right where he lived to cowboys and their families. He and Toni together knew they were to open their big log home on their ranch for that work.

He was not sitting beside Jesse Brandon now by accident. With God, there are no accidents. Only purpose. But he had to let God's Spirit show him how to minister to his friend, who was in some obvious distress. So he waited.

Finally, it was Jesse who spoke. "Judd, my insides feel like I rolled this truck over on myself. Everything in my life is changing...and not for the good. It's overwhelming with so many different things falling apart at once."

Jesse spent the next ten minutes pouring himself out to the only man he would have dared to confide in so personally. He told him about the decline of the ranch, even after praying so fervently for business to pick up. He told him about Matthew Parker, then about Laura and Andy. He didn't expect any real help from his cowboy preacher friend, but it did seem like his load wasn't near as heavy after he emptied himself out.

Judd nodded his head and waited a minute to let his thoughts form, then spoke them. "Jesse, you've been walking with the Lord for what...three or so years now? You've been coming right here to this house for church gatherings real regular. You've been growing right along...from a newborn child of God...to learning to become a more mature man of God." He paused a moment. "I believe God's bringing you through a big ole growth spurt, buddy. I don't know why it has to be painful but most of these real serious maturing times feel like we got stuck under a rock crusher. I'm telling you this from experience, Jesse. I've been where you are now. And I can tell you for certain...when it feels like all your pieces just splintered in all directions...try to keep remembering that God has a plan for you in it. He's teaching you something."

"Like what? How to act like everything's wonderful when everything's actually going straight to hell?"

"He wants you to learn to trust Him...to just stand still in the middle of your storms and look only to Him to bring you through. And I can tell you...that's never easy for us prideful men. He loves you, Jess, more than your human mind can fathom. I promise you...He *does* have answers for all of this...waiting up ahead of you."

Jesse stared at nothing out the windshield, trying hard not to break down in front of Judd.

"You may not realize it," Judd continued, "but you didn't show up here by accident today."

Jesse turned surprised eyes back to his friend.

"Fact is, I saddled up my pony about an hour ago to head out to the back ninety and cowboy for a while this evening...but before I could mount up...I suddenly felt a strong stirring come over me to stay home. Kind of worried me a little. I tied Pardner up in his stall and went back to the house to check on my wife and daughter. They were fine, so I sat down and waited. When I saw your truck coming, I thought this might have something to do with all the activity over at your place the past couple weeks."

Jesse's expression went from intently listening, to a stolid, blank look. He blinked as his brain switched gears with what he'd just heard.

"What do you mean? What activity?"

Judd just stared at him for a long moment while he swallowed the urge to curse. *Big mouthed preacher,* Judd berated himself. "Well," he raked a hand down his face. "I didn't intend to go there, but fact is, Donny came to see me a few days back...Said Miss Martha and Mrs. Parker were doing some really heavy duty, uh...decorating at High Point. Seems he promised them he'd keep it a secret but he was afraid he'd made a mistake by not calling you at the start of it. He wasn't sure what he should do. Obviously, he decided to let it be."

Jesse was trying to envision a decoration change throughout headquarters. Maybe some fresh paint on the old kitchen or bathroom cabinets? That would probably sound like heavy duty to those two ladies. But it shouldn't have been that much of a worry to Donny.

"Well, I don't see that rearranging the furniture or a spot of new paint is going to help anything. My business is fairly gone...But don't suppose it hurt anything either."

Judd realized that Jesse didn't have a clue, but decided to practice a little wisdom and keep his lip zipped.

Jesse drove in at the ranch at 7pm. At 7:05pm, he was still sitting behind the wheel of his parked truck, his eyes scanning back and forth across the whole ranch yard behind headquarters. He'd noticed the *huge* pots of *huge* sunflowers that lit up the front steps of his house. He thought it was a nice touch to a drab old porch.

But this! Pots and barrels of flowers? Trees? Cactus? A patio? *Concrete* patio? Was that a hot tub setting in the middle of all—that?

When his eyes traveled to the pavilion which was also decked out with monstrous pots of cactus and other foliage, the corner of his eye caught the tops of several huge—*teepees?* "What the...?"

He opened his door almost cautiously and stepped out, stupefaction being the only emotion he felt. The place looked like they were expecting a visit from the president of the country. And where was everybody?

A loud baa jerked him out of his stupor. He didn't have a goat. Then he saw the pens built along the broad side of his barn. A small overhead entrance with a shingle hung in the middle that read, *Petting Zoo?*

"Welcome back big brother." The back door of the house slammed behind Donny as he, too cheerfully, came out to greet the ranch boss.

Jesse spun to face him. "Somebody better be doing some real fast talking around here. Why didn't you tell me about this?" He waved his arm angrily in the air. "Whatever *this* is!"

The usual calm, almost comical expression Donny was known for didn't waver in the least, spurring his brother's anger even more.

"Well!" Jesse snapped.

"Simmer down, Bro. I don't have any answers for you, but there are two worn out little women inside the house eating supper that could shed some light on it. Might as well try to be civil because it's been a butt-kickin couple weeks around here and the whole crew is a little tuckered."

Jesse looked at Donny like he had a third eyeball setting in the middle of his forehead. "And would that be *my* ranch crew you're referring to?"

"Yessir, one and the same."

Jesse spun on his heel and headed for the back door.

"Jess, wait!" The sudden urgency in Donny's voice stopped him. "Andy's in there having his supper too."

Catching his meaning, Jesse stood still, but the muscles in his neck and jaw matched the angry clenching and unclenching of his fists. "Anything at all you want to tell me first, Donny."

The younger Brandon looked up at the sky, then down at the ground where he kicked up some dirt with the toe of his boot. He had already agonized over this issue. No matter how many times over the past few days that the thought crossed his mind to call Jesse and tell him what was happening, something, *something* seemed to stop him. Finally he went to see Judd Luke for some council as to how to handle it. The council was simply, "Ask your Heavenly Father...what's up? Then wait and expect Him to answer you."

In the middle of that same night, Donny woke up suddenly knowing that someone had just spoken to him. It was a strange sound that seemed to come from the inside of himself that said *All Is Well.* And he knew...He had his answer.

Donny looked back up at Jesse's now red, furious face. "No sir...not a thing."

Just then a noisy and grateful interruption bounded out the back door. "Mr. Jesse! You're back...Mr. Jesse." The small body slammed into Jesse, as thin bony arms wrapped around his middle.

It took every inch of nerves in Jesse to swallow his anger and respond to this boy who more than ever needed to feel protected and loved. He needed a father. He knew Andy had become attached to him. Jesse had caught him once trying to imitate his long swaggering strides. He thought his sides would rip the afternoon he saw Andy sporting a mustache he'd

135

smudged across his upper lip with charcoal and a toothpick hanging out of the corner of his mouth. Jesse was rarely without a half chewed pick poking between his teeth.

He reached down and spread one hand across Andy's shoulders and the other covered his head and pressed the little boy close for a few seconds. "Hey, pard, you been keeping an eye on things around here for me?"

Andy pulled back and turned his face up to Jesse's. "Yes. Wanna come look at the petting zoo? Me and Mr. Walton and…"

-336 "Hey, Andy." Donny broke in, not sure that conversation was a good one at the moment. "Come with me. I need a fishing buddy before it gets too dark. We better hurry."

"Oh boy." Andy left Jesse in his dust as he flew past him.

Without a moment's hesitation, Jesse strode to the back door and entered the kitchen.

Laura and Martha sat opposite each other at the center island, used paper plates and coffee cups in front of them. Both glanced up as he entered. Neither spoke as his furious expression raked one and then the other. He knew his large frame and fury aimed at them was the reason they were wide-eyed and frozen, but he deserved to know what had been going on at his ranch. And he intended to get his answer if he had them both cowering under their chairs.

He stood as tall and straight as his body frame would go, both arms folded across his wide chest. He knew he looked intimidating, but that wasn't his aim. *Maybe a double murder!*

"One of you needs to start talking…right about now!"

Laura raised her chin in defiance, already having practiced in her head for this moment. "Would you like some coffee? Or a BLT? Kitchen's open!"

His glare would have killed a normal, sweet hearted little woman, but this was Cattle Annie and Little Britches reincarnated, two notorious females who rode the outlaw trails in the late 1800's that he was facing down. As he recalled the story, those two had given marshals and peace officers a full load of indigestion. He closed his eyes a second and when he opened them, the same glare penned Martha.

"Maybe you'd like to start this off?" He could barely speak through his painfully clenched teeth.

"No...she wouldn't." Laura stood up, refusing to let Martha take the heat that was all hers. "This ranch business is between you and me."

"Ranch business!" Jesse exploded. What *business* is this ranch to you?"

Laura's resolve to be cool and in control slipped down to second gear. She was just now gauging the fierceness of his anger. She glanced toward the back door, contemplating an escape route, just in case one was needed. It dawned on her then that it was dark outside.

Andy.

"We'll discuss this later. I have to check on Andy." She moved toward the door at the same time Jesse stepped in front of it and blocked her way.

"Andy's fine. We'll discuss it right now!"

"I beg your pardon." Laura's glare now matched his. She raised her forearm to push him out of her way when two hands clamped her upper arms and forced her backward a couple of steps before letting go.

"Donny has him." He stood his ground, his tone clearly implying he wasn't moving until he got his answers.

The urge to bolt suddenly seized her and she blamed that cowardly spell on the rugged, murderous face that was honed in on her small frame, one that seemed very breakable at the moment.

Only a moment ago, she and Martha were exchanging whines and moans of pure exhaustion from a very long, near couple of weeks of hard labor and little sleep. She had no idea how much work she'd bargained for until she was already neck deep. Bless Miss Martha's soul. How the woman had kept up the pace was beyond Laura. Many times, she didn't believe for a minute she could walk another step and Martha, who was twice her age seemed to run circles around her. But right this minute, she believed she could cover a mile at a dead run, no problem.

Jesse nodded toward the hallway. "Go to my office," he snapped as if he was disciplining a child.

Laura flashed a look at Martha, who, to her astonishment, was sitting there politely sipping cold coffee, not a concern line etched anywhere on her face. Somehow, that was comforting and she drew from the older woman's calm demeanor.

Chin up, Laura squared her shoulders. "I believe that would be *my* office," she declared as she turned on her heel and headed down the hall.

Jesse entered the office behind her and gave the door a shove, slamming it. He caught her upper arm and spun her around to face him before quickly clamping both hands on his hips as if he didn't trust himself not to strangle her.

"That's as good a place to start as any! What the hell do you mean by this is *your* office," he barked down at her. He couldn't remember the last time he'd used a curse word and regardless of the shaking anger he felt, he also felt sorry for letting one slip out. He blinked and swallowed, trying to douse a little control over the fury that consumed him. It didn't work.

But Laura's fear and anger had been replaced with a welcomed, unexplainable calm. She waited a moment before speaking, deciding the best way to handle this would be to run right through the middle of the old proverbial *bush*. Lay the bottom line right on the table. She looked him straight in the eye. "I know that Matthew bought into partnership with you on this ranch, behind my back, of course. I accidently ran on to the information in your, *our,* desk. John Baines verified on the phone that he had handled a property deal for Matt here in Wyoming...about the same time you would have bought this place. Of course, I can't prove it right this minute because the papers I found in this desk are not there now...But I'm sure you know that."

Jesse was not just stunned at what he was hearing. He was paralyzed. His mind raced back to the final conversation he'd had with Matthew concerning their partnering on a dude ranch. Matt had been furious with his wife, whom Jesse had never met until she showed up here just days ago. Or was it weeks. He had desperately wanted to join Jesse, to pick up where they had left off with their ranching dreams. But he reluctantly chose to allow his young wife to have her way, to stay in the city on the concrete.

But Matt did buy 200 acres adjoining High Point as an investment for his son, asking Jesse to oversee that transaction for Andy's benefit. Jesse thought that was why Laura came here in the first place, because she knew about the property he was holding in Andy's name until he reached age twenty-one. The same 200 acres he had just had John Baines to sign over to Laura, with a fervent prayer that she would do the right thing by Andy. And she thought Matt had bought into High Point. Good Lord in Heaven!

He suddenly realized that she was still talking. More like shouting at him.

"And never mind that this ranch is going under! You can't run a dude ranch, Jesse, without *dudes*!" Laura felt out of control. Where were all these words coming from? They just kept pouring out of her mouth as if a faucet had been turned on, even though her mind was shouting at her to cut it off. She wasn't even aware that tears were running down her face, already wetting her dusty shirt front. "And maybe it was folding because you were so eager to join my husband in lying to me. You both lied and..."

The clank of spurs running in the hallway grabbed both of their attention.

"Jesse! Jesse!"

Jesse whirled around at the same time the office door flew open.

Ben was hanging on to the door knob to slow himself down. "Jesse, something...coyote maybe, got in the outdoor run with Rebel Man. He broke part of the fence rail and jumped. Donny and Hank and Jack are saddling up."

Jesse immediately followed Ben out at a half run, leaving Laura to rein her spinning emotions back in place. She was fully aware that Jesse's stallion had escaped, and for the moment, she knew she could relax and pull herself together. But she wasn't fitting back in place right. Her thoughts continued to riot. She wasn't finished. More words needed to come out, but she wasn't sure what they were.

She headed for the kitchen, needing to find Andy. He was perched on a stool with a chunk of chocolate cake and a glass of milk in front of him.

Martha took one look at Laura's red rimmed eyes and took a couple of steps to block her from Andy's view. "I'll take care of our little cowpoke here. You go get some time by yourself...I figure the boys will all be out late tonight."

She lingered, hating to leave Andy again.

"Go on now, honey." She cocked her head toward Andy. "He doesn't need you like this."

Just then a clap of thunder made all three of them jump. Oddly, Laura thought of the patio chair cushions. "I better move the pillows."

"I already did that. It looks like a real storm brewing...Not a good time to be out chasing a scared stallion. But that's all them ole boys know how to do anyway. They'll be fine. Now you go on to your cabin. Get some sleep."

When she didn't move, Martha reached her arms around her and hugged her tight for a moment. "Now, you listen to me. You're worn out and you...*we* have a lot facing us tomorrow, not to mention next week. I'm in this with you, all the way... You know, like Bonnie and Clydette."

Laura didn't want to laugh, but couldn't stifle a chuckle. And Martha's, *we,* did help to restring her nerves a little. She nodded and then walked around the bar to plant a kiss on the top of Andy's head before she went out the back door.

There was thunder and lightning, but off in the distance. She walked toward her cabin relishing the cool and cozy hide-out that the darkness provided. Somehow it seemed to lessen the turmoil still roiling away inside of her.

She knew what had just happened to her in the office. Old memories of her and Matthew. Memories from way before she'd ever heard of J.D. Brandon. He had berated her almost daily, holding her hostage to him through fear of his outbursts and degrading insults. The flashbacks had erupted like a volcano in picture after picture in her mind's eye, while she shouted, whatever she was shouting at Jesse a few minutes ago. She had no idea what triggered this blanketed pain. She had so carefully forgiven Matt after he died and tucked the thoughts of her years with him way down deep. She thought they would eventually just be forever forgotten.

She recalled then how she had felt when Matthew had talked about selling out and moving up north to a ranch. Nothing in her growing up years with her mother had given her any idea what kind of life that would be other than isolated, dirty and smelly and everything on the inside of her screamed *no* at the mention of returning to such poverty.

Matthew had taken her out of the extreme poverty of her raising and settled her into a nice middle class lifestyle. He was an angry man, but she had decided that living with his emotional abuse was a small price to pay for sleeping in a clean, dry bed every night and wearing pretty clothes and eating fresh, sanitary food every day. Yes, it had all been worth it to her, especially since the day she'd learned she had a baby inside of her. That was the day she had allowed herself to admit that her own mother had physically and emotionally abused her. Her mothering instincts intensified to the point of mentally focusing on never allowing the poverty of her childhood to get near her own children.

That's all she really knew until her mom had become too sick to care much. Somehow Laura managed to finish high school and made do with handouts anywhere she could get them.

After doctors told her mother there was nothing they could do for her disease, she simply went home to die. Laura had done the best she could, especially while enduring her mom's last months of verbal abuse and refusal to allow anyone inside their home.

When Laura found her in bed, staring sightlessly at the wall, Matthew Parker had been one of the volunteer rescue team members that came to her home that morning.

Suddenly, she needed to get away, to shut off these memories. A sob rose up from someplace deep in her soul. She tried for a few moments to suppress it all, but to no avail.

Loud thunder splintered the darkness giving energy to the storm inside of her and she began to run. The big rain drops sprinkling her face felt good. The darkness felt safe. So she kept going. She ran down the path she and Martha had driven to the old line shack trip after trip hauling stuff until they had transformed it into a sweet, cozy and fully stocked honeymoon cottage. But she wasn't headed there. Her emotions were too raw, her thoughts too dark and confused. Clouds had blocked out the moonlight now. She couldn't see the road, but she kept going until there was no strength left in her legs. She wasn't conscious of time, only the need to wear out this emotional upheaval.

Finally, she sat down to rest against a large rock that jutted out of the ground in the middle of a field. The grass was damp and cold, but she didn't care. She thought she should be afraid out here in the middle of nowhere in the dark, but she wasn't. It seemed like she had been afraid of something all her life. Her mother's rages. Her husband's criticism.

For the first time in her life, she felt a measure of control. These past couple weeks, she had made some drastic decisions.

Actually she felt strangely compelled to do all she had done on the improvements of this ranch. Just the realization that she had taken charge of her own life for once, planning and physically working the plan, eased her panic somewhat.

Then it hit her like a thump on the side of her head. It was Jesse's anger at her that had brought all of this to the surface. He had made her aware of him, aware that she wanted to feel love, to touch it, embrace it. And tonight he was furious with her. His anger had conjured deeply buried memories, making her feel like she was back at the mercy of her angry mother and husband. And she had become hysterical.

She wasn't afraid of Jesse. Angry, yes, at the injustice of what he had done with Matt against her. But not fear. This time was different. She didn't cower at the idea of Jesse's fury aimed at her. She had felt strength. A justified strength.

Naïve. That's what Jesse had called her. There was some truth in that, all right, but not to the extent she had lived in most of her life. Surely she had wizened up enough by now to keep herself and Andy free of another's mistreatment.

Laura felt her heart sink suddenly. Truth was Jesse Brandon's opinion of her mattered. As justified as she might believe her actions on this ranch to be, she knew she could have gone about things in a more rational manner. Oh well. *Spilt milk.*

A shudder shook her at the sudden image her mind pictured of Jesse's smile. Of the twinkle in his eyes and the moment his lips had touched hers the night of Bett's wedding. He was certainly attracted to her and he was nothing like Matthew. The two men seemed to be worlds apart. Matt had been a real sweetheart to her until the day after he married her. Maybe that was a trait belonging to all men. She had nothing to compare. Yet, her physical body had never once responded to Matthew. Fear and then repulsion was all she ever remembered. She had never felt her heartbeat run away with itself or felt an intense wanting inside of her being, until Jesse. These thoughts made her ache inside now with a longing that was almost painful. A longing for Jesse.

Laura awoke with a start to wind and water slapping her face. She was stunned to realize she had actually fallen asleep out here. It couldn't have been more than a couple minutes, but the sky had burst wide open spilling out lightening, thunder and, now, a sheet of water. She jumped up and ran in long, leaping strides across the field to the path that a flash of lightening found for her.

The honeymoon cabin was the closest shelter. By the time she reached the little porch, her breath was coming in short spasms. She leaned against the door for a few seconds to catch a good breath, then went inside and shut the door.

She stood in the dark against the door gulping in more air and hating that a puddle was forming around her feet in her brand new cozy honeymoon cabin. She and Martha had spent more time and effort on this project than all the rest put together. She was freezing, but she couldn't bear the thought of getting everything wet and dirty.

She peeled off her drippy clothes, undies and all, and piled them together, then squeezed her hair out on top of them. She tiptoed, as if that would keep her from tracking water, to the log bench they had used for a bedside table and snapped on the small lamp.

Laura stared in awe at the warm golden glow that flooded across the whole interior of the cabin. She had purchased a king size log bed with mattresses stacked high enough that a three rung step-up was needed to get on top. The comforter and bed skirting was white on white with lots of quilted pillows stacked and lined across the whole width of the cedar log headboard. Rug runners, mini blinds and curtains added a splash of color in their own perfect blend of patchwork charm. Silk daisies were set in various containers of eucalyptus stems that gave off a sweet and soothing fragrance.

It dawned on her that she hadn't seen the finished product of this cabin at night, bathed in lamplight like this. *Wow!* She could live here.

The kitchen and bath were decorated in like manner and completely outfitted with all necessities as well as extra surprises. The silk flowers and artificial cactus in every room finished off the effect that oozed *cowboy romance.*

Donny, Hank and Ben had worked hard, solid hours helping her and Martha transform this old line shack in just a couple of days. But she knew even they would be amazed to see it in this light.

With that thought, it dawned on her that there was way too much *shine* in the room. She didn't have a stitch on and was freezing. She headed for the bathroom to check out a hot shower, soaking until she could pass for a lobster. *What a wonderful place to be, stranded in a storm or on a wedding night!*

Wrapped up in one of the two fluffy white bath robes that Martha had insisted would be a nice touch, Laura thanked her a half dozen times, out loud, as she hung her wet clothes on the benches and ladder back chairs in the kitchen.

She turned a small flame on one burner of the cook stove, then started some brew in the coffee maker. While she waited for her favorite hot drink to make, she put the bathroom back in order and dried the wet floors.

"Oh...I really hate this," she muttered softly a few minutes later. She set her full coffee mug on the bedside bench and stared at the huge, inviting, warm bed that looked like it belonged in one of those Heavenly mansions Jesse was expecting to live in some day. She pulled back a corner of the bed covering, careful not to mess up any more than she had to, climbed, *literally climbed,* in and propped herself up on a mound of puffy pillows.

After a few swallows of coffee, she set her cup back down, leaned her head back and smiled without remorse. "Oh yes...I really do hate this."

She closed her eyes and listened to the wind howling as rain screamed against the window glass. The big bed felt safe, even though a storm was raging outside and not even Jesse's God knew where she was tonight. She thought how much she had changed just in the past months since she and Andy had been alone. She hardly recognized herself at all since coming here. She felt like a cage door had been swung open to set her free. And she must have leaped out and ran for it because everything looked, felt, smelled, tasted and *was* different.

Oddly, though, she wondered that she could feel so set free when she hadn't even been aware of her captivity. There was a great big world out here and she didn't even know it. And only now that she had stepped out into, or run blindly, it was as if she had never lived before now. She had never loved, before now.

Who would have ever guessed that Laura Neal Parker would have ever taken such liberties to direct all the work that she had on this ranch—*her* ranch and actually enjoy getting dirty and sweaty. And fall in love with a *cowboy*. She knew that's what she'd done. Fallen in love for the first time. And maybe for the first time, she had set herself up for a broken heart.

Laura slid down under the covers as an image of Jesse and herself wrapped together in this big log bed quickened her limbs into tremors and her stomach into a tight ball. It was a long time before she slept.

***

CHAPTER SEVEN

Martha watched the crew ride back in and dismount. It was a little after 3 AM. She had seen the truck and horse trailer lights leave the barn about an hour ago and return just minutes ahead of the riders.

Andy had been tucked in hours ago, but Martha sat up waiting for Jesse.

The storm had passed through just after midnight. Laura wouldn't answer her cabin phone and when Martha ran over to check on her, found she had never been there. She had checked the barn and even the teepees, thinking maybe she got caught out in the storm.

When Jesse headed across the yard toward the house, she met him part way. When he noticed the worry lines etched so tightly around her eyes, he began filling her in, even before he reached her.

"Rebel Man's hurt...Cut up in barbed wire, but we got him home. Donny's calling Les now and..."

"Jesse..." she broke in, swallowing a rising panic. "I can't find Laura."

His eyes rounded in disbelief. "What do you mean...you can't find her?"

"I sent her to her cabin before the storm hit. She wouldn't answer the phone during the storm and afterwards, I walked around the place to check on the animals and things. I decided to peep inside her cabin to make sure she was all right. But it didn't look like she ever got there. Her bed was still made."

"Where's Andy?"

"Asleep here in the guest room."

Jesse turned almost a complete circle as if trying to decide which way to go first. "Maybe she ran into one of the other cabins...got caught in the rain."

"No, I looked in all of them. I even checked the teepees."

He raised his hat off of his head just enough to rake his hand through his hair, then settled it back on. If he had ever been this exhausted before, he couldn't remember it. The worry mixing with it wasn't helping.

He looked toward the barn where Donny and some of the hands were taking care of his injured horse. When his gaze went back to Martha, he was already moving toward the drive way. "I'll take the jeep and drive around. Martha, check those cabins again," he yelled as he jogged into the darkness.

She was across the road and almost running when it hit her. The honeymoon cabin. No. She'd never have gone there in a storm, in the dark, on foot. But she turned suddenly and ran after Jesse before he could drive away.

"The old line shack...Drive out that direction."

Jesse looked like Martha had run out there and thrown a bucket of cold water on him.

"Trust me on this, Jesse. It's the only place I haven't looked."

He drove away then, shaking his head at Martha. *Poor old woman. I guess she's having one of those demented moments.*

Jesse drove to every cabin including Laura's. He looked inside her SUV that was parked in her driveway, then circled the perimeter of the ranch yard twice. His stomach muscles had tightened. This didn't make sense. He stopped the jeep in the driveway and let the engine idle a moment.

Lord Jesus, show me something here.

He saw headlights turn into the ranch and recognized Les Kane's veterinary truck. Strangely he didn't feel overly alarmed about Laura, but decided he needed to get help to locate her. He started toward the barn when Martha stepped outside the back door of the house and jabbed her finger at the back side of the barn toward the gate that led out to the old line shack. He couldn't keep from rolling his eyes. *Good Lord! I'm going to have her head examined right after I get mind done!*

He shot through the gate and followed a muddy, but worn road in the direction of the old abandoned shack. Who had been driving a vehicle out here lately that would make a road so visible? And why was *he* driving on it now, besides humoring an old woman? After everything else that he'd seen since he got home this evening, *nothing* could surprise him. Not even his own idiocy.

He was, however, surprised at his calm demeanor as he slowly made his way through mud and slick grass. Wherever Laura was, he felt inside himself that she wasn't in any danger. Maybe he had embarrassed her or scared her and she was hiding out, even though that didn't sound like her. Come to think of it, he hadn't searched the barn. Nah. She wasn't the type to curl up in a horse stall or on a hay bale. Or was she? After what she had done to his ranch the past couple weeks, she could be Jack the freekin Ripper underneath that beautiful and deceptively innocent face!

But Lord Almighty, she actually thinks she's half owner of High Point. *That would be MY office,* he mocked her, remembering her saucy little remark.

Suddenly, he burst out laughing until he had to stop the jeep and lay his head on the steering wheel. He didn't want to laugh. Nightmares are not funny, but he couldn't stop. He laughed until he wiped tears away with the backs of his hands.

Laughter doeth good like a medicine.

Was that a scripture that just rose up in his mind? "I don't *want* to laugh right now...thank YOU very much," he said aloud. Then he doubled over again until he was out of breath.

He sat for a few minutes after the laughter died away, surprised at how relaxed his body felt. Maybe God was trying to keep him from choking a woman to death tonight. And then again, maybe he'd just gone and lost his mind!

He shoved the floor shift in gear. The old shack was just around the corner. He'd turn around in front of it and go back to the yard and do a more thorough search.

He could barely make out the outline of the shack as he rounded the bend, but when his headlights shone on the front of the building, Jesse simultaneously hit his brake and stared, bug-eyed and open mouthed.

The front door was freshly painted red. An old weathered and broken piece of board with writing painted on it hung by a piece of baling wire in the upper middle section of that red door. Was that daisies circled around the sign? He squinted his eyes trying to read it. *Honeymoon Hideout.*

His eyes moved to the long wooden box sitting underneath the window and filled with various colored wildflowers, then to a brightly colored rug lying like a welcome mat on the porch floor.

What in the name of Uncle Sam Hill had happened here? For the first time since he got home, he felt completely unnerved. His stomach was queasy suddenly. He hadn't eaten a bite since breakfast and it was nearly breakfast again. He was beyond exhausted. He had laughed like a silly school girl a minute ago and now his whole body had frozen into a mannequin-like state at this ridiculous image of his dilapidated old line shack. Maybe his truck *had* rolled on top of him.

He got out and stepped up onto the porch, surprised at how sturdy it seemed. Then he noticed the new rough cedar trim around the window and the door. He tried the door knob, not surprised when the door easily opened. He pushed it wide enough until the jeep headlights bathed the interior.

Jesse thought he was past being shocked. He stepped just inside until he could scan the full perimeter of the room. He took in the big log bed posts, various decorations around the wall and the homey kitchen area with a basket of flowers sitting in the middle of the old table. He actually smelled coffee.

Clothes? A pair of jeans and gray T-shirt, socks and a woman's underwear were draped over the chairs and benches around the kitchen table.

He jerked his eyes back to the bed and saw a human sized lump curled beneath a quilt. On closer inspection, he could see the top of Laura's fine blonde hair and by the sound of her slightly raspy breathing, she had no clue she had a visitor.

Taking an uneven breath himself, he looked down at the floor, figuring she wasn't wearing anything beneath the quilt and knowing he should leave. But the thing was, he didn't want to leave. At this moment, he didn't know exactly what it was he did want. He didn't need so many answers now. He pretty much had this little *takeover* of his ranch figured out. What he was going to do about it, God alone knew. Money had been spent here. Looked like a good sum to him. And how would she react when she realized her mistake. *Huge mistake!*

Jesse went out and killed the jeep engine and headlights. He grabbed a flashlight from under the driver's seat and went back in and shut the door. He had to get a few hours shuteye. Come morning, he'd finish the discussion they'd started at headquarters last night. At least here they wouldn't be interrupted.

The whinny of a horse mingled suddenly with voices outside. He should have realized Martha would have sent a search party when he didn't come back.

0 Quickly he went back out and quietly pulled the door closed behind him. Donny and Ben had ridden out.

"Everything okay, brother?"

"Yep...Laura's here. Tell Martha. How's Rebel Man?"

"Les stitched him up and left antibiotics for a week. He should be okay."

"Alright...You boys go get some sleep."

Both turned their horses and headed back without another word.

Once inside again, Jesse closed the door, then took a couple deep breaths, his hands resting on his hips. He glanced at Laura. She hadn't so much as twitched.

He walked into the back room using his flashlight. He had to lie down before he fell down. He wasn't a bit surprised to find the bathroom all gussied up and working and the sofa in the small back room was perfect. He pulled off his boots and stretched out the length of it. Sleep was nearly instant.

The cabin was still dark when Laura finally stirred, but she thought she could see just a hint of dawn pinking through along the edge of the mini blind. She probably hadn't been asleep a couple hours. After the long hours she and Martha had spent trying to finish their backbreaking projects, she really didn't need a sleepless night. She felt drugged with sleep, but nature was calling on that late cup of coffee she drank.

She slid her feet to the floor and made her way to the bathroom easily in the dark since she knew the room arrangement so well. The bathroom was built just inside the little extra room. Martha had insisted on donating a sofa she had stored in her garage, so they set it in the back for the time being.

She walked carefully past the couch so she wouldn't stump her toe. Then *wham!* She let out a shriek as she stumbled forward grabbing for the couch to catch herself. When two large hands closed around her waist, stark terror pushed a blood curdling scream out of her mouth. She fought like a rabid animal, pummeling her attacker with her fists, clawing, scratching and screaming.

"Hey...hey. Ouch! Crap! Damn! Jesse caught a fist in his right eye, then another in his mouth before he got a grip on her wrists. He was on his feet now and jerked Laura solidly up against him to stop her struggles and to save his own hide. She screamed again. Then again.

He was going to have to apologize to the entire Arapaho Indian Nation for waking up their dead that were buried on these grounds.

"Laura! It's me! It's Jesse!"

She became still, but her breath was short and fast. "Jesse?" she squeaked into his shirt.

Heart pounding, it took a few seconds to register the fact that she was safe and that her face was stuck in Jesse's chest and that the material of his shirt and jeans was scraping against her totally exposed front side. Thank God, or whoever, but why is he here? She hadn't managed to find her voice yet.

In the silent darkness, Jesse released her wrists and cupped her face. There was enough light for him to see her fear. She appeared dazed, in the grip of shock. A long thick robe barely clung to her shoulders. He pulled it back around her, but not before his glance took in the flawless creamy white body underneath, so beautiful it took his breath. He swallowed hard, then lifted her up in his arms and carried her back to bed. She was shaking and held on to him so tight that he lay down with her and cradled her against him. It took some maneuvering to get both of them settled on top of the mile high bed. She didn't loosen her grip until he had her tucked in tightly against himself.

"I'm sorry, Laura. I didn't mean to scare you like that. You okay?"

"I think so. Why are you here? What...what were you doing in there? I didn't know you were in here. I thought...I thought..." Hysteria was rising in her voice.

"I know, baby. This is my fault." He pulled her in a little tighter. "You're safe. I came looking for you when Martha said she couldn't find you." He began telling her the evening events, hoping to calm her nerves back to a normal level. Before he got past mentioning the decorated front porch, he heard that same raspy breathing. She was asleep.

A slow grin pulled on his lips. He continued to hold her close, while staring into the darkness.

After a minute, the humor of the whole situation faded from his mind. Everything about this woman he was holding in his arms had been confusing and infuriating up until her over-the-top revelation that she was a CO-owner of his ranch. She made more sense to him now, because she absolutely believed that. Exactly how he was going to break the news he had for her, he didn't know. He also didn't know how he would be able to function here or anywhere else without her in his life. Despite all, nothing had ever felt so right to him as laying in *her* honeymoon cabin bed with her curled up in his arms. But even if Laura felt the same way about him, God certainly was not going to bless a union between him and a woman who was a professed atheist. He knew the Bible said something about not yoking yourself with an unbeliever or something like that. But he felt so strongly that she needed him to protect her and love her. He needed her to love him. But he had failed at measuring up once before, to being enough for a woman he thought he couldn't survive without.

Andy. Little Andy was his last thought before he fell asleep.

The sun was bright and high when Laura eased away from Jesse and slid off the edge of the bed. She practically ran to make her overdue trip to the bathroom. Jesse was still out cold when she returned. She gathered her dry clothes and stepped back into the bathroom and dressed.

She had slept in Jesse's arms last night. She shivered suddenly, wanting to laugh, then wanting to cry. He had come looking for her? And just crawled into bed with her when he found her? She covered her eyes with her hand and began to cry. She couldn't make herself stop. Her whole body was trembling.

Then it all came back to her. She had been attacked! She fought with somebody. Somebody who was trying to hold her down!

"Laura?" Jesse rapped his knuckle on the door, then pushed it open slightly.

Her eyes grew wide at the sight of Jesse's face. *Oh my God, we've both been attacked!*

"Are you all right?" she shrieked up at him, then reached up to touch his oversized upper lip.

The horror that filled her eyes caused him to look in the mirror, a little afraid at what he might see. It was bad enough, he supposed. His eye was already black and swelled, matching his busted lip.

But when Laura continued to cry uncontrollably, he recognized the effects of shock. *Lord, where was his brain? How could he have let this happen to her?*

Once again, he scooped her up, but this time set her down in a straight backed chair at the kitchen table.

"I want to lay down. I'm so sleepy." She started to get up and head for the bed, but Jesse gently pushed her back down.

"You aren't going to sleep. You need to eat."

In minutes, he set a cup of steaming coffee in front of her, followed quickly by a plate of scrambled eggs and toast. She almost had it all devoured before Jesse could sit down with his plate.

She got up then and headed for the bed. "I need to sleep," she mumbled, before tumbling onto her pillow from the step-up.

He sat at the table and watched her for a long time. He knew sleepiness was part of the shock's effect. She was asleep before her head hit the pillow.

How had this fragile little city girl managed to take over his entire ranch? His ranch hands? His home? His business? His brother? His housekeeper? He glanced around the kitchen. His abandoned old line shack, for Pete's sake? All in just a couple of weeks!

He really needed to get some perspective here. The woman had acted purely out of a need to avenge herself. Okay, she had been deceived by her husband. At least that's how she saw it. But he had nothing to do with Matt's purchase of the adjoining property. He had simply agreed to do a favor for a friend. And somehow that favor had landed him in the biggest mess of his life.

She had certainly spent some dollars here, obviously thinking she was building *her* business up. He had been too dumbfounded to think much about it before, but the eye appeal of the improvements she'd made was not bad. He shook his head at his attempt to accept this blatant, arrogant and daring coup by a little spurned city girl gone wild. He needed to get his head screwed back on good and tight and deal with this mess. If that was even possible.

Just then he thought of Matthew. He remembered the anger and frustration of his childhood friend the day the two men had shook hands for the last time. Jesse shook on his agreement to see the deal with Andy finished. Matthew had shook Jesse's hand good-bye.

He got up and went to the door and snatched his black Stetson from a hook on the wall. He stood a moment, staring at the curled up form on the bed, sound asleep. His emotions were many and mixed, but the one that took precedence at that moment was anger. An old shoved down deep anger that had found its way back to the forefront.

He left. He would come back and check on her later. Right now, he had a mess to start cleaning up. As if he knew where to start!

Jesse sat behind his steering wheel in his driveway and once again took in the sights of what used to be his dude ranch. His old fashioned, back to basics dude ranch that had just been modernized to a city girl's way of roughing it, and by a city girl who was about to be given a real tough lesson in the perils of *leaping before she looks*. And right at this moment, he was more than happy to be the teacher of that lesson.

He pulled up to the side of the barn and went in to check on Rebel Man. The stallion was laying down in deep, fresh shaving, his front legs bandaged nearly to his shoulders. His side and hip that showed had gashes coated with purple goop. Jesse decided he would catch him standing later and examine him more closely.

Just as he reached the barn door to leave, Hank Walton stepped inside. Jesse was about to ask why he was so dressed up, but the old man's jaw dropping stare arrested his question. Then he realized why. He remembered that his face looked like he'd been whooped by a bear.

"Don't ask!" He growled at the questions he saw in Hank's eyes.

Hank gave an unsmiling nod, then stated, "We're about to leave for church. Don't suppose you're going this morning?"

Jesse took a step back and rolled his eyes upward. "I forgot it was Sunday."

There were some questions he wanted to ask Hank concerning the past days around here, but decided they could wait until later.

"Guess I won't make it today...but maybe you could do me a big favor." He pulled his wallet out of his back jeans pocket and fished out some dollars. "Put this in the offering for me...would you?"

"Okay." Hank folded the money and slid it into his shirt pocket.

The sound of Andy's voice, then Martha's sounded like they were coming to the barn. Hank caught the dart of panic that flashed in Jesse's eyes and caught on immediately. He didn't need to be trying to explain his busted face. The older gentleman backed out of the barn without a word. Seconds later the group was slamming pickup doors, headed for Judd Luke's Cowboy Church service.

It lightened his mood some to see Andy all slicked up and headed for church.

Jesse walked around the grounds, amazed all over again at the new face his ranch was wearing. The hot tub with all the pots of cactus and flowers and the patio furniture with huge red umbrellas over the tables was—well, it was eye catching.

Two large pens of goats were contentedly munching hay. A couple of baby lambs were in the mix and Jesse had to reach over the gate to rub each one on the head. PETTING ZOO was emblazoned on a huge cross board in bold red letters, creating an entrance gate to the area.

The pavilion had taken on a more festive atmosphere, but those teepees took the cake. He walked into what looked like an authentic Indian village. But when he looked inside the dwellings, he was totally stunned. Some had furniture inside including fully made half beds covered in Indian blankets and rugs on the floor. But one teepee that faced slightly away from the circle and away from the others nearly did him in. Inside was a full size log bed made up with faux skins and Indian blankets. Huge *skin* covered pillows were on more Indian blankets on the floor; a small chest of drawers with a dressing mirror on the side of it and a battery operated lamp decorating the top. And, of course, a big basket of assorted wild flowers.

He headed back to the house, glad to find some strong, black coffee still in the pot. He heated a cup in the microwave and went to *his* office. *HER office, my butt!*

He sat down at *his* desk and worked hard to get his anger under control. He thought about talking to God about all this, but was too mad to go there.

He yanked his hat off and tossed it across the room. Just as he raised his cup for a sip of the steaming coffee, the phone rang and he sloshed it on his *big* lip. He put the cup down and grabbed the receiver with every intention of throwing it against the far wall. Instead, he answered it.

"Hello. May I speak to Laura Parker?" It was a very young sounding female.

"She's not available. I'm Jesse Brandon. What can I do for you, young lady?"

"Well, my husband and I, we were just married this weekend. We wanted to stay in your honeymoon cabin next weekend but Mrs. Parker said it was already rented. She said she had an Indian teepee that was very nice and fully furnished and everything and it was very unique and would make our honeymoon very special...so is it still available for next Thursday, Friday and Saturday?"

Jesse sat frozen, even after the long winded little bride had run out of air. *The honeymoon cabin was rented next week? A teepee for a special...?*

"Hello?"

"Uh, just a minute." He finally unlocked his tongue. "I'm checking."

The guest schedule book was lying beside the phone. He turned a page, then another. Every cabin was scheduled for guests next week! He didn't see anything about a teepee, so he reserved it for the newlyweds.

After hanging up, he jumped up and paced back and forth across the room. *Was ANYBODY planning to tell me ANYTHING that was happening here?*

He tried to remember that in the Bible, God promised He would never leave or forsake him. He also tried to remember if the Bible said anything about the twilight zone!

He stopped ranting suddenly and stood up straight. It just dawned on him that, according to the schedule book, he had a ranch full of people coming in a few days. There was always preparations to make, scheduling of daily events, groceries to buy for the chuck wagon and making sure the hands knew what their jobs were each day.

He stepped to the desk and looked at the book again. Six cabins loaded with families. More than a dozen kids and half as many adults. And now, there was a petting zoo to man and a hot tub with safety issues for children.

He raised up and raked a hand through his grimy hair. One thing was for certain. This day would not be over until there was a huge meeting of the minds of all people involved with this ranch.

But right this minute, he needed a really long, hot shower.

-336

An hour later, Jesse decided the moment of truth had come. He rapped a couple times on the Honeymoon Hideout door before he opened it and stepped inside. A pile of linens stripped from the bed were on the floor beside it. He peeped around the door and found Laura sitting at the table. He walked in and sat down across from her.

After a few moments, Jesse broke the silence. "I'm sorry about last night. I should have woke you up when I found you...and I shouldn't have kicked off my boots in the middle of the floor.

Laura shot a *so that's what I tripped over* look at him.

"But," he continued, "that's the old 20/20 hindsight for you."

She nodded at him.

"I'm glad to see you feeling better because we need to have a real serious discussion right now. I took a tour around my ranch this morning." His tone was flat.

She let the *my ranch* go by. "So, what do you think?" She tried to sound cheerful, but her tightening stomach muscles said the conflict was on.

"What I think is that you have a lot of explaining to do." His gaze turned stony.

"Well, what a coincidence. I was thinking exactly the same thing about you! And since I already clued you in last night at headquarters...why don't you begin by telling me about yours and Matthew's *secret* partnership on this ranch. I know you're smart enough to realize that everything Matt Parker owned now belongs to me."

"Well, there are different types of laws and rules for most things...so that's debatable since you obviously don't have all the details of the transaction. But, let's just say you are half owner of this ranch. Where did you get the idea that that fact would entitle you to do the things you did here without consulting the owner of the other half?" He crossed his arms and leaned back in his chair.

Angrily, she stood up and leaned toward him, both palms flat on the table. She had to strain to keep her voice below a shout. "Maybe you should back up a few years and remember why you had no qualms about partnering with my husband to deceive me...to lie to me and now you're trying to steal what belongs to me and Andy. I deserved better...Andy certainly deserves better than that!"

Now Jesse was on his feet. His tightly controlled anger had escaped. He jabbed a long finger toward her face. "*You* back up and get a few facts straight. You discovered some paperwork for a land deal with my name and Matthew's signed on it by snooping in *my* personal files where you had no business being. Am I right?"

"I was trying to..."

"Yes or no?" he barked.

She lowered her eyes. It wasn't exactly like that, but he wasn't going to hear her.

"Fact number two. You were so enraged over discovering Matthew had made a decision without your knowledge...one that involved me...you figured yourself out a way to get back in *control!*" Jesse felt something come apart way down deep inside of him. He was surprised at the tightening in his chest. Suddenly all the anger he had swallowed for years came up and poured out of his mouth.

"And the real fact of the matter is...you detest this ranch and the lifestyle that goes with it. You're a city girl to the core of yourself...so damned devoted to demanding your own way, a luxury filled life, you couldn't see there was more to loving a man than having him grovel at your every whim, to the point of refusing to share a little bit of his dreams. Lifelong dreams, Laura. Matt was like an older brother to me when we were growing up. He said you demanded that he give up our friendship if he wanted to keep you and his baby son."

Her mouth dropped open in disbelief.

He continued baring his soul. "And being the man he was... he did the honorable thing. *That* I can truly respect him for. But you didn't even have the decency to let me know he was dead. He was gone three months before I even knew."

Numbness settled over her. None of his accusations were true. Maybe a small, but misunderstood part. She *had* demanded that Matt stop talking to her about moving up north to live on a ranch, but Jesse didn't understand why she couldn't go there. She didn't hate this ranch or the lifestyle. She'd seen and experienced more of life here in the past weeks than she knew existed.

She just now began to realize how much Matthew had meant to Jesse. And maybe she was guilty of robbing her husband of his dreams, to some extent. But Matt had not been a kind man to her. Not from day one of their marriage. He was a bully. A control freak and jealous, even of Andy. She also knew that she would not reveal that to Jesse. There was no need for him to know.

His words had cut her to the core of her heart. The pain was brutal, but she remained quietly numb.

He had walked around the corner from the kitchen and stopped, but she could see him. His shoulders appeared slightly slumped forward. One arm held his weight as it rested on the small mantel high above the cold fire pit, the other hand resting loosely in his jeans pocket.

Finally she forced words out past the pain constricting her throat. "You don't know how it was with me and Matt, Jesse. You want to hurt me the way you think I hurt him. I wasn't strong enough to leave the only real home I ever had...The home Matt gave me."

She walked over and stood just a couple of steps from him, his back still to her, but she could tell he was listening.

"Have you ever lived in a two room shack that dripped rain...soaking your bed at night...freezing in the winter until you thought you couldn't possibly live through it? Did you ever do without food a whole day at a time...hoping that wouldn't turn into two days? I never knew a dad and I don't remember a day in my mama's life when she wasn't sick."

Her voice came only in a whisper now. "Do you have any idea how it feels to see your mama lying in an ugly box and not be able to do better for her. Matt gave me a chance to do better. He gave me a warm dry place to sleep and good food every day. I was afraid to let it go. I had to hold on to that security no matter what. I didn't want Andy to ever know a day like I lived."

She stopped and was silent for a moment, then, "I never meant to hurt anyone," she whispered sadly.

A wave of compassion settled over her for the big powerfully rugged cowboy who still stood with his back to her. She wanted to comfort him. Slowly she went to him and placed her hand lightly on his arm. He didn't pull away like she expected, but turned towards her. Her heart shattered as the moisture from his eyes welled into pools of deep suffering and she realized then that Jesse had not truly mourned his lifelong friend's death.

He reached for her and slowly drew her to him. She wrapped her arms around him and they held tightly to each other for a long time.

***

CHAPTER EIGHT

Finally, Jesse released her and took a step back. She let her arms fall to her sides. When she looked up at him, he looked different. There were no harsh lines in his face. It was peaceful, but still he looked uneasy.

Without a word, he reached into his back pocket and pulled out a legal sized white envelope and handed it to her.

She turned it over, but there was no writing on it. "What's this?"

"The truth," he said quietly, then walked to the door and went outside to sit on the edge of the porch as the door shut behind him.

Laura pulled some kind of document and a letter from Jesse out of the envelope and read both papers without moving a step. The letter spelled out very simply everything her husband had done in purchasing two hundred acres adjoining High Point Ranch, put in Jesse's name until it could be signed over to Andy on his twenty first birthday. Jesse had deeded the two hundred acres to Laura, *fully trusting you to carry out Matthew's wishes for his and your son,* the letter said.

She slapped her hand over her mouth in an attempt to stifle a gasp as the truth sank in. She got to the step-up beside the bed and sat down hard as her knees went to jelly.

"Oh my God!" she whispered between her fingers that covered her face. Everything that she had done on this ranch, Jesse's ranch. "Ohh." She moaned in pure agony of embarrassment. Of shame. How could she ever look Jesse in the face again? And Martha. Everybody at the ranch. She felt sick to her stomach. She wanted to die. She was shaking when she felt Jesse's presence towering over her. She hadn't heard him come back in. She dropped her hands into her lap, but she couldn't look up. Humiliation had dropped her with both barrels!

Jesse bent down and picked up the papers and envelope off of the floor. She didn't know she had dropped them.

She stared at her hands in stunned misery. "I don't know what to say," she whispered.

"Well, for starters, I'd like to know how much money you spent on this upgrade of my ranch." His tone wasn't angry, just matter-of-fact.

She looked up at him then. "I don't know exactly. I'll have to figure it up. You...you don't need to worry about that now...I will..."

"I didn't plan on worrying about it," he interrupted. " I deal in facts and I want the facts."

That cut, but there was no place to argue with him. "I'll get a total for you and leave it on your desk. I'll be leaving as soon as I can get packed up."

Jesse stared at her for a long moment with wide eyes. "Aren't you even a little bit curious about a two hundred acre spread you just became owner of?"

A blank look crossed her face, "I'll think about that later. Right now, I just need to..."

Run and hide is what she was thinking. Get away from enduring being the laughing stock of this whole ranching community. Oh, God. She wanted to die.

After a long tense silence, Jesse squatted down in front of her and gathered the small work roughened hands into his. She tried to pull free, but he held tight. The intense pain in Laura's eyes brought compassion in Jesse's spirit that overrode his anger at her.

This was a woman who hadn't deliberately done anything, probably ever, to hurt another person. With Matthew, she had simply responded to life out of the horror of her raising. And whether she ever admitted it or not, he knew her life with Matt had not been that great. Andy's revelation to him and Donny on one of their fishing excursions had been a little tough to swallow at the time, but Jesse knew Matt wasn't what he should have been to Laura or Andy. *'I'm glad my daddy lives in Heaven, cause now my mom doesn't cry anymore. Mr. Jesse makes us happy.'* The remembrance of Andy's words that had been directed at Donny that morning, coupled with the devastation now washing Laura, body and soul, threw a better

174

perspective on this whole circumstance. The building and rearranging of his dude ranch could be dealt with easy enough, in time. But suddenly, the one thing he knew he couldn't deal with was losing Laura.

"Let me tell you what you need to do right now," Jesse said.

Laura bit her lip to stop its trembling. Even though Jesse's tone was carefully gentle, she dreaded what he was about to say.

"Look at me, Laura."

As hard as it was to do, she met his gaze.

"Here are the facts. You've taken it on yourself to create several major events here and then you scheduled a full calendar of guests to arrive in a few days from now. I do not have the manpower here to manage it. I need extra hands... Yours and Martha's to start with. And," he added with emphasis, "I'm not *asking.*"

She gaped at him in horror. "No Jesse, I can't face everyone...I just can't."

"I didn't say you had to volunteer any information. No one except you and me knows what the truth is about this. Let's just keep it that way...then there won't be any reason to feel uncomfortable."

"You would do that for me...after...?"

"I don't see any need to make things worse than it is. What's done is done. We just need to get organized and take care of these customers the best we can."

She didn't know what to say. The whole climate had changed for her. High Point Ranch had nothing to do with her life. She was a guest, the same as any other visitor. She had been so sure and so full of herself the past few days. Back breaking days. And it had all served no purpose other than to take her to her knees in shame.

No matter how hard it would be to leave this cabin and continue as though nothing had changed, she owed Jesse that much. Eventually she and Andy would go home and resume their lives far away from the judgmental looks and laughter that was bound to come. And how long it would take after that for her to hold her head up again, at the moment, felt like never!

She pulled her hands out of his and simply nodded her agreement.

Jesse stood up. He moved a hand toward the laundry on the floor. "Leave that. You and Martha can put this cabin in order later. I'll take you back to your cabin so you can have some time to yourself before I call a staff meeting at Headquarters this afternoon."

"Andy must think I've deserted him."

"Andy went to Cowboy Church with Martha and Hank this morning. He's in good hands."

"Cowboy Church?"

"Judd Luke has church services in his home on the Double OO Ranch."

Through Jesse's calm factual attitude, he had taken over the driver's seat, not only with her, but with Andy, as well as the running of his ranch business. And it was oddly comforting.

She took no issue with Andy attending a church. He was too young to understand or care about what was preached at him. She nodded and went out and got in the jeep.

Jesse's heart squeezed at the censored self-condemnation not only in Laura eyes, but in the way she walked. It killed him to see her hurting like this. There was no more anger or suspicion leveled his way, but witnessing her dejected spirit was far worse. He knew what that was like. There were no words or actions, even from those closest to you, that could lighten that despondency. He was just getting the extent of how his inexcusable anger toward her since she had been here had contributed to her state of mind now.

As justified as he had felt in his behavior, he hadn't known until today, the scope of who Laura Parker was or what she had experienced in her young life. He tried to recall what Pastor Judd Luke had taught a few weeks ago: *The rough edges of our adult behaviors stem from unresolved issues from our young lives.*

He looked out of the open door of the cabin at her as she sat as straight as a mannequin in the jeep. She had no idea how beautiful she looked, even through the visible scars on her soul that he could see so plainly in her eyes. The magnitude of his part in that, his crudeness and anger, hit like a huge fist in the middle of his gut.

Laura hadn't expected anyone to come out to the Honeymoon Hideout when she heard a truck motor just outside and a door slam. In seconds, the vehicle left.

Jesse had agreed to let her skip the staff meeting and take his jeep back to the old cabin to clean up the mess they had made. The Hideout's first newlyweds were coming in just a few days.

She had taken a long, leisure shower after Jesse dropped her at her own cabin earlier in the day. She and Andy spent most of the afternoon engaged in some serious mom/son time, ending around 4 PM after a swim in the creek.

Andy had been indoctrinated during church that morning with some Bible story about Jesus healing sick people. He kept bringing up the story to her. It was no more than any other fairy tale he had learned, but for some reason, this one irritated her. She had always listened to his endless rambling about Peter Pan and enjoyed his silly imitation of him. But it rankled her nerves with this Jesus character and finally, after several attempts, got Andy off the subject.

When Laura encountered Jesse after returning from her and Andy's swim, he hadn't hesitated a second before responding favorably to her going back out to the cabin to clean it up. She didn't know what Jesse planned to tell everyone, but she just wasn't up to sitting in on it.

He had quickly agreed, but it was plain to Laura that Jesse seemed to be only half listening to her. He was distracted, mumbled that the keys were in the jeep, then he stalked off to the barn.

Andy and Pup loaded up in the back seat, where Andy fell asleep before rounding the last curve to the cabin. Pup seemed content to lay on the seat at Andy's feet while Laura went inside and set to work.

Before she could look out front to see who had driven up, Martha walked in. Laura's insides twisted, figuring her loyal sidekick knew the scoop now that the staff meeting was obviously over. If she could wiggle her nose and disappear, she'd be on the other side of the globe right now.

But Martha had a big smile for Laura. "Ever heard of a sight for sore eyes? That's what you are. Don't scare this old lady... Bad for the ticker."

Laura almost laughed, but swallowed it, knowing she referred to her disappearance during the storm. "Sorry about that. I just meant to take a short walk but..."

"Yeah, doo-doo just happens...don't it?"

Laura did laugh then.

Martha scanned the interior of the cabin, then clamped her hands to her hips. "Looks like more than doo-doo happened in here."

"I swear, it's not what it looks like."

"Well, that's disappointing! Maybe next time...huh?" Martha bugged her eyes out toward Laura.

Laura chuckled and threw an armload of dirty laundry at her.

"At least we know now that the food supplies we stocked in here and the leftovers from feeding our hungry workmen wasn't such a premature idea after all," Martha surmised further as they restored the kitchen back to its re-do.

In short order, the cabin was back to clean and cozy, except for washing the bed linens and towels. Martha had not asked any questions about her and Jesse's obvious night together nor did she let on that she knew Laura had made an idiot of herself over the ownership of this ranch. In fact, if she knew, she was one fine actress. Not one word or look gave Laura any indication that Martha was aware things had changed. Maybe Jesse meant it when he said he wouldn't give her up.

After the women loaded up in the jeep, Laura was backing away from the cabin when a towhead popped up over the back seat almost sending Martha out the window.

"Hi, Granny Martha!"

"Oh...you!" She laughed and tousled hishair. "I didn't know you were in here."

A small giggle escaped through his hand that covered his mouth. "Pup's in here, too."

Martha craned her neck enough to see the collie contentedly curled on the backseat. "Well, I should have guessed she'd be here if you were, kiddo."

"Granny?" Laura glanced at Andy, then back at Martha, then remembered telling Martha she could consider herself Andy's honorary grandmother, or something like that.

"Yeah, Mom. She's my...my..."

"Stand-in Granny," Martha helped him out.

"My sh...se...can you just be my granny. I can't say all that."

"Okay. Granny it is."

Laura glanced at Martha and saw her eyes fill up, then jerked her eyes back to the road.

"Well, just don't cry...cause then Mom will...and..." Andy pulled a face and rolled his eyes before falling back into his seat. "Oh brother."

Both women laughed out loud and mopped the trickles of salty drops off their cheeks.

Laura parked the jeep as close to the back door of the house as possible and helped Martha unload the laundry.

Les Kane's veterinary truck was parked at the barn. Probably checking on Jesse's horse.

Martha gathered up the bundle and shooed Laura away. "You go relax or something. I can do this and while the laundry's going, I'll see what we're doing for supper. I don't need any help...Go on now," she said before a protest could be made.

In seconds, Laura found herself standing beside the jeep, not a soul in sight. She had seen Andy and Pup disappear around the barn door, so figured she'd better go there first to round him back up.

Not sure who knew what about her now, her nerves were dancing a jig as she entered the semi dark building. A light shown inside one large stall about middle ways of the barn. She could hear a male voice, but it was too low to understand what was being said. The dog was standing outside the stall door in the ally and staring hard at where the voice had come from. She didn't want to intrude on the goings on in there, but she needed to get Andy out of the way. His curiosity would have taken him right to the center of the action.

Before she would have stepped inside the lighted pen, Andy came out, head down and crashed into her.

"Whoa...where are you headed in such a hurry?" Laura clamped her hands on his shoulders as he tried to get around her. "Wait a minute...Hold on." He was wrestling with her.

"No, I gotta go...I have to hurry. Let go, Mom." Andy wiggled free and ran for the barn door, Pup shadowing his heels.

Laura stared at the door as it shut behind the pair. She decided he probably almost waited too long to head for the bathroom. Case solved.

She started after him just to be sure everything worked out all right, but a vaguely familiar voice stopped her.

"Hello, Mrs. Parker." Les Kane nodded his hat at her as he headed for the door, both hands full of plastic tubes and various doctor stuff. He paused a moment. "Your boy was just here if you're looking for him."

"Thank you...I saw him." Then she quickly added before he could walk on, "How's the horse doing?"

Les stopped and took a couple slow steps back toward her, shaking his head. "Not going to make it...I'm sorry to say."

Laura's eyes widened with shock. "But...but I thought he was getting well...What happened?"

"Don't know. Rebel Man picked up some strain of bacteria that took him down quickly. Fluids...antibiotics...nothing helps. He's almost bled out internally. Never saw anything happen so fast. He might have an hour...maybe two."

Laura felt like she'd been kicked hard in the stomach. Rebel Man was Jesse's pride and joy.

Les walked out.

Laura stepped back to the door of the stall and saw a sight that would be imprinted in her memory for the rest of her life. Jack and Ben were backed against the far wall. Two other hands that Laura had only seen at a distance were standing up against an end wall, all with hats off and hearts lying at their feet.

Jesse was on his knees at Rebel Man's head, stroking the stallion's neck and face. His big, wide shoulders were slumped over as though to envelope his sick friend in the closest circle he could get to a hug.

Donny was squatted on one knee beside his heartbroken older brother, a hand resting on his shoulder while Hank stood a step behind Jesse, hat in hand.

Laura stepped to Rebel Man's back where he was prostrate on the stall floor, signs of blood in the straw bedding and matted in his tail.

Jesse's pain filled eyes met Laura's and held for a moment. Hot tears burned in her eyes, overflowing at the corners. She wanted to drop down beside Jesse and gather him into her arms. She wanted his pain to stop. No one spoke a word, just stood or knelt in total silence. Waiting.

Suddenly, Laura remembered Andy. Quietly, she left, no one seeming to notice. She fought hard all the way to her cabin to swallow the choking lump and stop the flow of tears. Her heart was broken at the sight of Jesse and everyone of his big cowboy *family* barely holding themselves together. Jesse was their rock. That was so obvious, the respect that each of these men had for him. Seeing him kneeling and broken, saying good-bye to his beloved horse, brought the entire ranch to his side to stand broken beside him. Laura leaned her head against the outside of her cabin door and wept.

Some minutes later, she went inside calling for Andy as she quickly checked out the cabin. He wasn't there.

When she walked into the kitchen at Headquarters, Martha took one look at her face and froze. Laura told her, through a fresh overflow of tears, about Rebel Man.

"Oh Jesus...help." Martha rubbed her hand across her eyes and shook her head at the devastating news.

"I came to get Andy," Laura stated simply.

Upon learning that Martha hadn't seen Andy or Pup since they got back from the Honeymoon Hideout, Laura took off outside as fast as her legs would go, Martha right behind her.

Laura ran afoot to the creek, while Martha yelled all over the ranch yard for Andy and the dog.

But, Andy and Pup were missing.

Les Kane drove slowly and heavy hearted back toward the Double OO Ranch's bunkhouse where he lived. He knew Jesse Brandon's ranch family would see him through this ordeal. The scene in that barn was too painful for him to hang around. The memory of the mistake that had cost him his vet practice back in Missouri was still too raw. A mistake that had cost him his fiancé, a woman who had stolen the heart and soul out of him, then kicked him to the curb. He had made a terrible mistake, all his fault, and he would pay for it the rest of his life.

"What in the name of..." Les couldn't believe his eyes. His mental anguishing came to an abrupt halt at the sight of little Andy Parker and Jesse's dog walking down the road in front of him. Holy smoke! They were a solid two miles from High Point.

Les pulled over and honked his horn. By the time he leaned across the seat and shoved the pickup door open, Andy climbed in without preamble and immediately stated his case.

"Hi, Mr. Les. Could you take me to see Jesus? I need Him real bad."

Les sat back at the little boy's words, forgetting all about chewing on him for wandering off. "Well, do you know where you can find Him?" Les asked, trying to get at where Andy was headed in the first place.

"Yeah, you know...At the big pretty house where that man said that Jesus lived with him."

Judd and Toni Luke's house.

"Please, Mr. Les. We have to hurry up."

"Sit tight a minute."

Les got out and went around to load up the collie in the narrow back seat. By the time he got back behind the wheel, Andy's eyes were tearing up.

"I think we better get you back to your mom, because she..."

"No! Please...please. I have to go get Jesus...Please take me."

Against his better judgment, Les headed for the Luke's. He could call High Point and let them know where Andy was and maybe make some sense of all this.

"Okay, Andy. We'll go talk to Preacher Luke."

"Can Preacher Luke get Jesus?"

A chuckle burst out of Les. "I bet he probably can."

Five miles later, Les and Andy stood in the foyer of the Luke's house where Les told Judd and Toni what he knew.

Judd squatted down to Andy's level and looked the little boy in the eye. "Andy, would you mind telling me what we need to talk to Jesus about?"

"Mr. Jesse's horse. You know...Rebel Man. He's sick and Mr. Jesse's real sad. Jesus has to come and make him well."

Judd and Toni exchanged glances with Les.

"You said Jesus healed all those people cause they asked Him for help, so I want Him to come heal Rebel Man for Mr. Jesse. Can you tell Him to come?...Rebel Man will have to go live in Heaven if He doesn't come."

Les explained about Jesse's stallion. "He only has an hour or so left in him...if that."

Judd suddenly began to get emotional. His hands were shaking. He was being called out on his own sermon that Jesus was our healer if we would only ask. And by a five year old child. What was he suppose to do with this?

Judd put his head down and squeezed his eyes tightly shut as if to relieve some pressure. When he looked back up,

Andy's wide-eyed innocence was patiently waiting for an answer.

Judd cleared his throat. "Tell you what, son. You go with Mrs. Luke here and have a cookie. By the time you've finished it...I'll be ready to help you with this."

"Okay."

Toni and Andy headed for the kitchen and Les stepped into the office to use the phone to call High Point Ranch.

Judd went down the hall and into the master bedroom. As quickly as he got the big double doors shut and stepped down into the sunken privacy of his favorite room in the house, he dropped to his knees and immediately began to seek his Father with more fervency than he'd ever done in his life.

Father God. Oh, my Father. Did you hear what that child said to me? He actually believes that I can take Jesus over there and get that horse healed. You know that I can't heal that horse. If You don't show up and do a miracle...then I can't do anything.

Judd groaned from way down deep as though in great pain. His entire body shook to the point he thought he might be having a heart attack.

Father, that child listened to me teach about a healing Jesus. And he believed. Lord, what are we going to do? I'm not moving from this spot until You tell me what to do.

Judd was bent over, face to the floor now. He waited, but only for what felt like seconds. Almost immediately he seemed to be watching a movie. The scene was of himself getting out of his truck at the barn at High Point. He watched himself walk inside to a stall and saw Rebel Man prostrate on the ground. He noticed the horse was barely breathing. Then he watched himself walk in and kneel down at the stallions head. He laid his hand with his fingers splayed across the side of the sick pony's face and said, "Bleeding stop! Body...function the way your Creator made you to function. In Jesus Christ's Name...Rebel Man, get up!"

Then the movie was over and he found his face was still bent to the floor of his bedroom. He simply stood up. These words moved through his mind then, *I can do nothing, except what I see the Father do.*

As if wings had sprouted on his feet, Judd flew out and down the hall. But when he spoke, he very calmly said, "Come on everybody...Let's go."

Except for Les, all loaded up in the Luke's crew cab truck, including Pup. Les decided he'd had enough trauma for the day and drove around to the bunkhouse.

When Andy asked where Jesus was, Judd simply said Jesus had asked him to go in His place. Strangely, that satisfied Andy.

The few miles to High Point was the longest and most tormenting drive of Judd's life. No one knew what had just taken place in that bedroom. Judd wasn't even sure he knew. What he did know for a fact was that he was strongly compelled to head for Jesse's barn. At the same time, his knees were knocking and his mind was screaming at him to turn around before he made a total fool of himself. *You're going to embarrass your whole family. No one will darken your door again to hear you preach. Turn around. Who do you think you are anyway? Your credibility is about to be destroyed by a five year old kid.*

Judd wanted more than anything to drop this kid and dog off at High Point and drive right back home. He also wanted more than anything to have enough faith in his God to just go do what he was shown. To believe God had actually shown him that vision. To know and not doubt. To not be shaking so hard with fear that he had to swallow again and again to keep from puking.

In the end, the Luke's vehicle unloaded at the barn door. Andy ran ahead and entered the stall at a run, his face beaming. Martha had delivered Les's message of Andy's whereabouts, so the entire ranch was there with Jesse and Rebel Man.

Laura shot Andy a, *you're in a heap of trouble,* glare, but he never even noticed.

Jesse respectfully stood up when the Luke's entered. He shook their hands and nodded, but said nothing.

Judd had settled the issue in his heart when he got out of his truck. If he couldn't trust Almighty God, then he needed to quit preaching. But it didn't stop his stomach from heaving or his legs from wilting.

Judd looked around at the wall full of cowboys, then down at the stallion whose breathing was so shallow, he couldn't see his side moving. He couldn't seem to move or speak. Then, everything began to happen.

Andy announced that Jesus had sent Preacher Luke in His place to make Rebel Man well.

"Come on." Andy grabbed Judd's hand and pulled him closer to the horse.

Judd focused on the prostrate horse, even though he could feel every eye in the barn widened and on him.

"Andy!" Laura's shriek came out in a whisper. She recalled immediately the story her son had told her over and over that morning. Something about Jesus healing sick people. She was mortified! What had Andy done? And what had these religious nut cases done to her son?

Laura reached out and grabbed Andy's arm to get him out of the middle of this mess. Before she could begin her retreat with Andy in tow, Judd stepped forward and took charge.

"Wait...please." He looked down just a moment as he silently prayed for courage. His heart was about to jump out of him. "I know this all sounds off the wall to you folks...but this young man is right. For some reason...God showed me He was going to do a miracle with Rebel Man. Either I've completely lost my mind or God surely did speak to me in a vision this afternoon."

Judd was trembling so hard he wasn't sure he was speaking clearly. He had just put his entire life, family, career, reputation on the line with these people. *God help me!* Not a soul had moved a muscle and none seemed to be breathing any better than the horse.

He squatted down in the same place Jesse had been and started to put his hand on Rebel Man, then stopped and looked up at the lineup of shock faced wranglers on the *feet* side of the horse. Without thinking, he simply said, "You boys move to one end or the other of this pen...You're in a dangerous spot."

Amazingly, they quickly vacated that whole wall.

Judd laid his hand on Rebel Man's face and spoke clearly the words he had heard during his vision. He closed his eyes and finished..."In Jesus Christ's Name...Rebel Man...get up!"

Judd felt something bump beneath his hand and heard several gasps around the pen almost simultaneously. He opened his eyes just as the stallion suddenly rolled up off of his side to rest on his belly, gathered his feet underneath himself and stood up.

Judd came to his feet and jumped up in the air with a shout. "Yeah! Whooo...Thank You, Jesus!"

Andy bounced up and down like he had a trampoline under him, before grabbing Judd around the hips. The kid couldn't grin any wider. There wasn't any room left on his face. Judd lifted him high and bear hugged him before setting him back on his feet.

Jesse stood still staring wide-eyed at Rebel Man, not realizing tears were running down both of his cheeks. He glanced toward the door at Laura. She was shaking her head, her face frozen with shock and fear. When she saw Jesse look at her, she ran.

He wasn't surprised or alarmed at that. He was a believer in God and His miracles, but had never seen anything like this. It was taking every cell of his flesh to keep him on his feet. His knees had lost strength. Laura was a confessed atheist. Of course she would run.

Across the bloody straw covered floor, Ben was on his knees openly sobbing. Judd was on his knees beside him, with an arm around his heaving shoulders. Ben had always scoffed at the idea of Cowboy Church. Until a few minutes ago, anyway. Martha and Donny were hugging each other, half laughing, half crying. It was pandemonium in this stall and Rebel Man was taking it all in stride. He had shook himself, then began nibbling tiny pieces of alfalfa hay off the floor, ignoring the commotion surrounding him. He also seemed to be in excellent health, except the barbed wire gashes were still visible.

Jesse noticed Andy had disappeared. He didn't feel a need to look for either him or Laura. Awestruck was all he could feel.

He finally got his legs to cooperate and paused a moment to pat Rebel Man on the rump, then walked outside. He walked and walked until his emotions overtook him. He was a quarter mile cross country, nearly to where Laura's property joined his. What he had just witnessed would have been hard to believe if he hadn't seen it with his own eyes. Even at that, it was hard to wrap his brain around it.

With arms hanging loosely by his sides and his shoulders slumped, Jesse looked out into his earthly view of the heavenlies. His voice was low and throaty. *"Lord, how do I say thank You for something like this? You visited my ranch...my home."* He lowered his face and stared at the blurred ground. He didn't know what to do now, but he did know he would never be the same man he was before this.

Then he remembered the prayer he had uttered to God, asking that He would show Himself to Laura somehow. Prove to her that he was real. Is that what just happened? She couldn't deny the reality of Almighty God now.

***

CHAPTER NINE

Fortunately for Laura, the past few days were full with no time to think—much. She should have packed up and gone home, she berated herself. What was it going to take to get her away from this place? *Hail balls sailing upward from the ground?*

She had worked hard to shove the memory of what she had witnessed in the barn three days ago out of her conscious thoughts. She'd spent most all of her down time in the Headquarters office, closed away from the invariable talk about a miracle of God. She couldn't put a name to what had happened, so ignoring it altogether was her best answer. The only problem was, she wasn't able to ignore it altogether. Something strange happened, that was for sure. But she just couldn't think about it. She *wouldn't.*

The ranch would be filled with guests by tomorrow and everyone would be too busy to talk about it.

She was seated behind the office desk to monitor the phone for a while. Her eyes closed for a moment's rest and suddenly and very clearly she saw an image of Rebel Man raise up from near death to instantly stand up, alive and strong. Then, just as suddenly, she covered her faced with her hands and cried.

Jesse slid the saddle off of Rebel Man after a short ride to the creek. For three days and nights, he had fought to shut out the horror he'd seen in Laura's face as she witnessed his beloved pony's miraculous healing. He didn't know how to approach her. But he did have the answer to her question concerning *why* he believed in Jesus. He had gone to visit the cowboy preacher yesterday and was shown in the Bible the very simple answer to that and the answer was the reason that he knew he had to give Laura some space. As much as he wanted to reach out, to talk about what happened, he could only watch her from a distance and wait.

There was no doubt that he had fallen, not only into a more humbled place before his God, but he'd fallen into a hopeless pit, head over heels in love with Laura Parker. He refused to visualize his life without her in it.

But they were as different as red and blue. He was from the old school of ranch life, simple and unsophisticated. He had rough edges about him that he knew wasn't attractive to women. Most days, he was dirt caked and poop splattered. Animals had to be tended and doctored, at times around the clock, inconvenient or not. And this was simply who he was.

But Laura needed, no, she deserved to be loved by someone who would lay his life down for her. God knows, she had borne her cross her entire life, whether she realized that or not.

Jesse knew from the bottom of his soul that he could show her what it was like to feel secure and well loved, something he knew she'd never experienced with anyone. He wanted her. She was the air in his lungs. Every breath he sucked in was fueled by a thought of her. He would leave ranching for her if that's what it took.

He finished up in the barn and when he stepped outside into the bright sunlight, a sudden acute awareness rolled through him. Somehow he knew he needed to find Laura. Whether God was moving him or just his own demented desire for her, he couldn't tell, but he took off to the house just shy of a run.

Martha and Hank were in the kitchen surrounded by stacks of food and paper goods, preparing for a week of chuck wagon cooking. After one look at Jesse's face as he hurried through the door, Martha smiled and pointed toward the office.

How did she know these things?

He opened the office door and walked in unannounced. The door gently clicked shut behind him.

She looked up, but sat still and waited for him to say something.

Jesse stood in the middle of the floor. He couldn't seem to move his feet or his gaze away from hers. His heart glittered like fire in his eyes, completely unconditional, uncovered, bare bones aching emotion.

And she saw. The purest of love danced and sparkled with open abandon straight into her deepest soul until she felt all of her resolve, all arguments, all self-control shatter and crumble away. This very moment she knew she couldn't hide from the truth any longer.

The truth was, this man knew a God who was real. And she wanted to know his God. And the truth was, she wanted this man as much as she could plainly see that he wanted her.

Without breaking the intimacy of their locked gaze, she got up and without hesitation walked into Jesse's waiting arms. For a long moment they melted against each other, clinging tightly and relishing the rapturous feeling of holding on to someone you are desperately in love with. His arms pressed her like a vise, her face against his chest.

Jesse was breathing hard and his heart felt like it was about to blow apart. He could feel her heart beat racing with a rhythm that matched his own.

If Laura had ever in her life felt safe and wanted and alive and loved before this moment, she didn't remember it.

"Jesse." She pressed tighter against him as she whispered his name that was so precious to her.

He stepped back enough to bring both hands up to cup her face. He smiled into her eyes as his thumb moved as light as a feather across her lips.

She was dying for his lips to touch hers, but he continued to study her wet emotionally charged baby blues and letting her savor the passion and the joy that filled his.

The tenderness that they shared in those moments felt almost other worldly to Laura. Never did she imagine such intimacy could be enjoyed in such a way. She drank from the rich depths of his gaze until she knew she was loved in a fullness almost beyond her comprehension.

There was no need for words. Jesse had wanted to say *I love you. You're mine. We belong together forever.* But instead of uttering those words out of his mouth, they poured from the deepest core of his being, straight through the window of his soul and into hers. Something too wonderful for words had just happened. He could feel a powerful love coming from his depths and loving Laura with a pure, untouchable intimacy.

He asked her then, even though he already knew the answer. "You know God is real...don't you?"

She nodded as fresh tears spilled over.

Then he lowered his head and kissed her deeply and passionately until they both had to come apart for air.

A desperate hunger, longing, need began to stir her body in a way she had never felt before. She wanted these strong arms around her for the rest of her life and she knew she was about to say the craziest thing that could have ever popped into her head. Confusion stirred through her intense desire to give herself to Jesse, and the new and profound knowing inside of herself that there was a real and living God watching.

Jesse saw the perplexed flicker cross her face. His hands massaged her neck and shoulders as he focused solidly on her. "What's wrong?"

When she hesitated, he coaxed, "Tell me what you're thinking."

She tried to look away, but he held her. "Well, I just...sort of wondered if your God would not like what we're doing. I mean...like how I'm thinking and feeling...that I want to do with you right now."

Jesse nearly let himself choke on his own saliva before he could cough it up and swallow, but laughter crinkled in his face. Only the serious, wide-eyed look he was getting helped him hold himself together. He wanted to ask her exactly *what* it was she wanted to do with him, just to hear her say it. But he full well knew. It was in her eyes, her kiss, her rapid breathing and Lord, he wanted to do the same thing with her right now.

But he sobered up quickly as he let what Laura had said sink in. It was obvious she had experienced a real change in her spirit that set Jesse back on his heels as the realization hit him. This was Laura Parker, the atheist, who was worried whether God would disapprove of their hugging and kissing. The reality of who God is wasn't there for her yet, but the fact that she was thinking in such a way spoke louder to Jesse than what a whole year of church sermons had accomplished for him. He suddenly felt it imperative to tread lightly with this new believer's heart.

He was torn. There was a sweet song in his heart. A praise of joy for Laura's spiritual awakening. And there was a wild aching need to haul her trembling little body into his bed and make love to her until the sun rose, and rose again, and again, for decades to come!

"Come here," he whispered and pulled her against his chest and rested his chin on top of her head. "I believe with all my heart, Laura, that God Himself sent you straight up here to me.

You know I want you. My feelings are flashing in neon off both my sleeves."

He sucked a long breath, then moved back enough to look at her expression. "I want you to live on this ranch with me. I want you side by side with me every day and in my bed every night. And I want to be a daddy for Andy." He paused, giving her a chance to process his words.

She felt a fluid-like wave of peacefulness wash through her whole body at his affecting words. Before she could question his intentions, he told her plainly.

"I love you, Laura. Give me the chance to show you how a man ought to love a woman...How a husband should love his wife."

Her eyes grew wide and so did her mouth.

He grinned down at her. "Say something."

"Yes."

"Yes?"

"Yes, I'll marry you. I love you...I want to spend the rest of..."

His lips came down none too gently on hers. After a long minute, he raised up and tilted his head back and took a loud, throaty, exaggerated breath of air, then bent down for a second go.

A giggle bubbled in her throat and broke up the kiss. She squealed as he lifted her off the floor and whirled her around in a circle. It was hard to believe all that was happening to her. Marriage to this beautiful, loving hunk of a man that she just happened to be nuts about.

She'd never been in love before. That was an obvious fact. And the love she saw in Jesse's eyes when he looked at her was an unmistakable fact as well.

"How about we get married tonight?"

He was so serious, she was momentarily shocked into silence. Her eyes were so wide they ached. "I *know* you're just joking."

He pulled his lips into a slight smile, his eyes squinting with mischief and slowly shook his head.

"But, Jesse, that's impossible!"

"The only thing standing in the way is your *but, Jesse.* Where's that *git her done* sense of adventure you're so famous for around here." He was laughing now, but serious as a rattle snake bite. "We could sneak off before anyone caught on and..."

"Jesse! Listen to yourself...You're not making sense."

"Then let me clarify myself." He drew her closer in against him, tightening the grip of his arms around her. He gazed down into her face with pure unashamed sincerity. "I love you, lady. Every tiny thing about you. You're more important to me than my own life...I would lay it down for you, Laura."

"Jesse..."

"No...I'm not finished. I want to show you from this second on what it feels like to be truly loved. I want you to feel safe and know that there's somebody looking out for you and that little boy in there. And I want your warm little body in my bed tonight as my wife. And I..." He froze mid-sentence as it dawned on him that tears were in her eyes and that he had probably just won the *self-centered-man-of-the-year* award.

He brushed at a salty drop on her face with his thumbs, then kissed her gently. "I'm sorry...baby. Lord Almighty...I can't get past the marriage proposal without making you cry. That was selfish of me. I know you would want a nice wedding."

It took a few seconds before Jesse saw it. There was a sudden gleam, a mischievous gleam in her eye and it was aimed up at him.

"And so...*where* did you plan on us getting married at this hour?"

He was startled at the look she was giving him as she asked the question. Was she serious?

"Uh...I know a preacher right up the road."

"You want to elope...up the road?"

"Elope? Sounds like something a couple of naughty kids might do."

"Does...doesn't it?" She shifted her eyes and grinned and he caught the dare with all the devilishness of his few-years-gone youth.

He wasted no time. "I'm going to make arrangements for Andy with Martha and you slip out the front...go to your cabin and pack an overnight bag and..."

He stopped cold when Laura pulled away from him, leaned back against the edge of the desk and laughed with pure delight.

"What? Aren't we serious? I thought..."

"Yes. I'm as serious as you are. But don't we need a license? And are you forgetting about all the dudes that are coming tomorrow? There's no time for this."

Jesse hung his head. "I *really* want to cuss right now," he said to the floor. He stood up straight and pulled his hat lower on his forehead. "Well, it sounded like fun, anyhow." Jesse couldn't keep his disappointment from showing. "We'll talk about this later. Right this minute, I have to *make* time for a long...*cold* dip in the creek...thank you, mam!"

With a teasing crabbiness, he strode out of the office, mumbling to himself, but where Laura could hear him. "Who ever heard of not having time to elope?"

Laura couldn't keep from giggling at his little mock tantrum. She was disappointed too, but happiness at what had just occurred in the past thirty minutes of her life over ruled even that. She was dizzy with a ridiculous giddiness. She was so in love with Jesse. She had only fantasized about how that would feel, never being sure that there was such a thing. But now she knew. She was going to become Laura Brandon.

It occurred to her then that there were a lot of things to do. She had to go back home and pack up her things, put her home up for sale. What would Andy think? Should there be a wedding? A wedding ceremony strangely didn't appeal to her. She just wanted to be Mrs. Jesse Dane Brandon as simply as possible and get on with this wonderful new life. She couldn't have dreamed this life up for herself if she'd had a lifetime to do it. It almost seemed as though this 360 degree change in her's and Andy's lives had been pre-ordered or something.

Like it had been there all the time and they had just stepped over into it.

Laura had never experienced such a heart swelling happiness in her life. The closest she'd ever come was the moment she had laid eyes on Andy's little wrinkled newborn body. But that was a separate kind of joy from what she was feeling right now. Her newborn son had meshed her heart and soul together to a place of being needed and that need became her single reason to want to wake up every morning. Her reason to live.

But Jesse. He had taken that bound part of her and Andy and infused a wild strength, a power, a total infusion into her heart, soul and body. She didn't just need to get up every morning and live. Her insides seemed to be exploding with life itself. This had been growing on her ever since she had first seen Jesse come riding into the ranch yard from a trail ride her first day here. She'd been falling head over heels for him since that moment.

But there was more to it than all that. Since the instant that Jesse's horse had stood to his feet, in place of drawing his final breath, something else had happened inside of her. Something more than a euphoric, madly in love with Jesse happiness. No. She knew that she knew, there was a God. Strange, unexplainable things happened all the time. True, she had never witnessed such a thing before, but she'd read stories. God was truly real. She knew. She just didn't understand why she so totally *knew* that.

SURRENDERED II

Jesse wasn't kidding and he didn't slow down until he was fully submerged, head and all, in the roped off swimming hole in the creek. His brain hadn't been fully engaged since the day that little blonde whirlwind blew into High Point. Most of his thinking and reasoning powers had gone to a more *southern* part of him. This was not his first flying leap into cold water since—Laura.

He was thankful to Jesus that she hadn't cut and run after her first day or two here. If he hadn't come up with that *job* at Headquarters for her, he knew she would have run for Texas by morning. But not in his wildest did he see coming from her what came. Seems she had all this *taking care of business in one huge boundless sweep* personality covered up completely. He doubted *she* had even been aware of who she really was, the love and the joy and the go-getter attitude that was imprisoned on the inside of her.

Obviously she'd never bonded with a dad or her mother either. And Matthew. He didn't want to believe his best friend from his youth had turned out to be a jerk to his wife and child. But Jesse recalled the fact that Matt had acted a little weird when he'd asked questions about his family. He could see it now. Matt deliberately had kept him from meeting his wife. Maybe he was afraid Laura might recognize that she was missing out on something sweet. Loving. Kind. Matt had been a troubled kid. Jesse knew that about him. Maybe his pain went with him into his adulthood, marriage, fatherhood. Jesse shook his head. He couldn't think about that now. No point. Right now, Laura was his point!

He groaned and squatted to submerge himself a full half minute beneath the water. When he stood up, he sucked a deep breath of air. He was standing in a hole that made the water nearly chest high. The last time a woman had gotten under his skin this deep, he was one week away from the alter when he lost it all. Jilted was an understatement. He was crushed. Katie had left him hurting until he had rudely refused the attentions of many young *play-like* cowgirls that had passed through High Point. Now, here he was again, only in worse shape than before.

Laura was nothing like Katie. Even thinking to compare the two made him want to laugh.

Katie was a flirt, but he'd never seen it as a real threat. He wasn't, by nature, a jealous man. That was just Katie, so he thought. But when one of the neighboring ranch hands took her up on her flirtations, she dumped Jesse, all the wedding plans and left the state with him. He did laugh then and silently and profusely thanked that cowboy.

Laura, on the other hand, was not just under his skin. That woman was overheating his blood veins. She was unspoiled, unpretentious, nervy, unbound, passionate, which all spelled sexy. And, she was in love with him. No room to doubt that! His stomach jumped and quivered every time he thought of the night he'd spent in the old line shack, a.k.a. the Honeymoon Hideout, holding her nearly naked and trembling body through most of a night. Longest few hours he'd ever spent in his life! He'd had to literally pray his way through that one! Never, ever had any woman, even Katie, affected him this way. He had become a mushy, demented, disturbed excuse for a man. It was all he could do to move around the ranch and keep a little dignity about him. If it was the last thing he did, he would find the time, way soon, to get this woman married to him. He groaned again and took another long dunk under the water.

Laura had never in her life experienced true exhaustion before the few days just passed. Neither she nor Martha realized the work load of their upgrade on the ranch activities when the place was filled with guests. Laundry duty for the cabin bed linens and towels was overwhelming by itself. Then there was the hot tub and garden area to service. The food service from kitchen to chuck wagon kept Martha busy helping Hank and the petting zoo had to be watched with so many young kids running around. Even Andy ran to and fro acting as a go-fer for whoever needed something *got.*

Between the trail rides and hay rides and manning the swimming hole, Laura only caught glimpses of Jesse and Donny throughout the week.

The honeymooners out at the cabin had access to a golf cart that Donny drove in from somewhere to move themselves from the cabin to the ranch yard, although they didn't show up often.

Every available hand was kept busy until late every night. One cabin was not rented out in order to be used as a bathhouse for the teepee campers.

Laura and Martha had beamed like proud mama's when the ranch reservations had filled to capacity. And now, six days later, they were even prouder when the last car of guests waved good-bye and drove out.

It was Saturday night and two totally done-for wonder women sat at a table on the patio and shared a whole pot of coffee and some exhaustion induced hysterics. All Laura and Martha had to do was look at each other to break up laughing. What a week! One more like it would kill them both for sure.

Andy was fast asleep in Martha's room where she had coaxed him to spend the night with *Granny*. It wasn't hard to get that done.

The men were still congregated in the barn taking care of horses and zoo animals. Except for a small pile of sheets and towels in the laundry room, everything had been cleaned up and readied for the next guests.

Laura had not allowed herself more than a couple times an hour, all week to think about Jesse's marriage proposal. Those twice an hour thoughts kept her able to put one foot before the other when her energy was failing her. She'd had to nearly bite her tongue off all week long to keep from telling Martha. She wanted her and Jesse to make the announcement together. And as much as she wanted to talk to her best friend and partner in crime about it right now, she would wait. She really wanted to wait. Oh, what the heck!

"Martha, I have some news to..."

"Well, there comes the dude wranglers now." Martha half shouted over Laura's head, obviously not interested in hearing her news.

"What are you two up to?" Jesse asked.

"Nothing special...A little girlie talk," Martha chirped. "You boys hungry? I can put on a fresh pot of coffee...if ten o'clock is not too late for you."

Hank and Donny walked up behind Jesse.

0   "Nothing for me, Granny." Jesse picked up the new tag for Martha after hearing Andy call her that all week. He could tell it suited her justfine. "A long sleep is what this old body needs." Jesse walked directly behind Laura. "How are you holding up, young lady?" He rubbed the side of her face with the back of his hand and Laura would have reached up to cover his hand if he hadn't kept on going, not even waiting for an answer. "Hot shower and sleep is all I can think about right now." Jesse spoke into the air in front of him and disappeared inside the back door of his house.

Laura only half heard the other two men's replies. She stared at the back door of the house where Jesse had so abruptly disappeared, evidently for the rest of the night. She wanted to follow him, but he hadn't invited her. Everything but!

For the next couple minutes, Laura worked hard to shut out the confusion and lump in her throat that Jesse's behavior put there. She knew he had to be bone tired like they all were. But his rudeness made her think he had decided he'd made a mistake and just didn't know what to say to her now. She got up and muttered goodnight. No one heard, but kept visiting amongst themselves.

She dragged a heavy heart and aching muscles across the lane to her cabin. After a hot, sudsy shower, she thanked God out loud for that wonderful thing called a bed and fell in.

It was the dare that did it. Those baby blue fire balls that Laura had shot his direction a week back when he'd suggested what she termed, an elopement. It didn't seem like his little plan had been spoiled for him. The ranch was dead quiet, except he thought he'd heard some moving around coming from Martha's room. He worked as quietly as possible and retrieved a ladder, well, a step stool from the utility room and carried it across the drive to the side of Laura's cabin. It was just after midnight when he placed the stool on the ground under her bedroom window and tap, tap, tapped on the glass pane. He didn't figure they'd had enough drama at High Point yet. So he was just doing his part. HeeHee.

"Laura," he whispered as loud as he dared and rapped louder with his knuckles. She was either going to kill him dead or marry him—tonight! Jesse had planned this all week long. Even snuck off to Jackson and managed a marriage license and a ring without Laura's knowledge. His little brother had stood in as proxy to sign for Laura. Some crazy rule that Judd Luke had told him about. Judd and Toni were waiting at their place for them right now to perform the *I do's*.

"Laura." Tap, tap. "Wake up, baby."

"Wh...what the..." She rose up on one arm and blinked the glue out of her eyes. "Jesse?"

"Yeah, it's me....Open this window."

She raised the mini blind and stared at him as if his head had changed into a nut laced fruit cake.

He grinned and tapped the glass pane again. "Open the window."

Laura clicked the lock open and Jesse pushed the window up for her. "What on earth are you doing?"

"Get your clothes on. Whatever you want to elope in...I've got a license, a preacher and a witness waiting on us."

He watched her face begin to crinkle until she couldn't hold it any longer. She giggled, her entire face pink and suddenly filled with that same mischief he'd seen the last time he tried to get this done. "But, why are you at my window. I have a...a door."

Her laughter was the sweetest sound he'd ever heard in his life. "Because we're e-lop-ing. Look." He pointed down toward his feet.

When she leaned out the window and saw the step stool waiting on her, she couldn't stop the squeal of disbelieving laughter and eagerness. Her legs danced a jig in place with the impishness of a daredevil teenager.

Before she could pull her head back inside or close her wide open mouth, a flashbulb went off in her face from the darkness. "Oh, Jesse...you're an idiot!"

"Well, you better hurry up so you can marry this idiot before the preacher goes back to bed."

She wheeled suddenly, still giggling. A night light shown under the bathroom door giving her light to see to grab a pair of red silk lounge pants and a white V-neck tunic. She ducked into the bathroom and changed.

When she came out, Jesse was leaning over the window sill, forearms resting in the window, hands clasped. He wore a white western shirt, the top two pearl snaps undone and a black felt Stetson. He was grinning like he'd just won the lottery.

"Grab your toothbrush...That's all you need," he instructed her.

She got it and poked it in her pants pocket. In another few seconds she was astride the window sill when another camera flash went off.

"Please tell me that's *not* our wedding photographer out there."

"Oh, but it is. Don't do anything...goof-ball...or she'll have it all documented."

She! "Martha," Laura bellowed into the dark spaces, "just wait till I get home, young lady."

A familiar chuckle sounded from behind a big pine tree.

Once her feet stepped off of the stool, Jesse grabbed her hand and they ran for his truck, flashbulbs popping behind them. Laura was happy about the pictures because when the night was done and she had time to think, she'd need the proof to believe she had done this.

***

CHAPTER TEN

It was after one o'clock in the morning when Mr. and Mrs. Jesse Dane Brandon drove away from the Luke's beautiful log home and headed for a little getaway lodge on another end of the Luke's property. Jesse had been fishing in the private lake many times and remembered the homey log lodge that sat nearly on the water's edge. Judd rented it out to friends that needed a break from the big city life. He and Toni had graciously offered it as a wedding gift for a honeymoon for the next three days before another round of dudes would arrive at High Point.

The short ceremony had taken a while to get done after Jesse and Laura told them their elopement tale. The laughter was hysterical and finally, weakly, Judd pronounced the couple husband and wife. Toni signed the license as their witness and snapped a few pictures to go with their priceless beginning.

Judd was still chuckling as the newlyweds went out the front door. "Only the Second Coming could have made me miss this night," he quipped to his wife as the door shut behind their neighbors.

Nothing in Laura's wildest imagination could have conjured up a wedding event like this. Nor would she have wanted anything different. The whole plan was so her. And who knew? If she'd been asked a week ago what her dream wedding would be, it certainly wouldn't have been this. She would have described something traditional and *likely*. Not this. But this night held every sweet, endearing, nutty dream for her that brought out her true self. The man sitting beside her now, who had slipped the delicate little diamond band onto her finger tonight, her husband, in all of his wacky, prankster, sweet, God-loving ways brought more happiness into her insides than she ever knew was out there to be had. How had something this wonderful just up and happened to her? These things happened in movies or romance novels. And here she was living the happy ending. Except she and Jesse were just beginning.

Laura didn't have a clue what the scenery was outside. Darkness swallowed everything except the rough road directly in their headlights that wound through dense pines until it opened into a clearing.

Jesse pulled up beside a beautiful log structure that resembled a miniature of the Luke's big home. Silver twinkle lights were entwined down the center posts of the long covered porch and along the banister on both sides. Laura dipped her head slightly to see inside through the windows as several lamps glowed like gold on the rich log interior.

"Wow! Look how gorgeous." She exclaimed softly.

"I am looking." Jesse's voice was low and husky.

Laura looked up and watched his gaze settle on her lips. She met his gaze with a smile and Jesse trembled with sheer anticipation of the night that lay ahead for them. It seemed he'd waited for this moment his entire life. And he fully intended to make every second count, not only for himself, but for his wife.

He had almost made two life altering mistakes. One, by baring his heart and soul to the wrong woman. Jesse longed for love, from this *one,* beautiful, spirited, innocent little city-gone-country girl that didn't mind getting dirt or poop under her nails and who was clearly going to be a hot babe in the sack. Only this *one* sitting beside him. No other would do. Ever. And, *thank You sweet Lord,* she was his wife.

Before he let loose with the loud wooo-whooo that was yelling inside his head, he smeared a long, wet kiss on his woman's lips and opened the truck door.

The lodge was the most romantic place Laura had ever walked into. The lamplight cast a warm golden glow around the den. There were at least five lamps burning in the one room. A red leather couch and matching loveseat sized chair centered the room in front of a stone fireplace. A red and tan braided rug pulled the cozy cottage effect all together. Various candies and fruit filled a large wooden bowl on the lamp table beside the chair. A gift box and card with an over-sized yellow bow was stuck to the envelope. Jesse opened it and read the card aloud: *Congratulations Jesse and Laura Brandon. Eat, drink, be merry and anything else that suits your fancy. Kitchen and bathroom are fully stocked. Enjoy! God's Blessings, Judd and Toni.*

Laura lifted the lid on the box to see a beautiful red leather Holy Bible with, *Jesse and Laura,* embossed in gold letters on the bottom of the front cover.

After a stunned minute, "It's pretty. I've never owned a Bible."

He looked down into her face at the strangeness of her whispery soft tone. He could tell she was genuinely touched.

"My name is on it, Jesse." She lightly touched the gold lettering with the tip of her finger. "Our names."

She was subdued at the sight of her name on the Bible. Something was stirring inside of her, a disturbance she didn't understand. It was an unpleasant feeling. An unworthiness.

He saw her discomfort and took her hand and squeezed. When she didn't respond, he knew something was going on inside of her that he needed to step back from. He turned around and brought up a small gas flame in the fireplace. Nights were always a little chilly, but he was opting for atmosphere as well.

"Why don't you get comfortable, baby. I'll go scare us up a couple cups of coffee." He squeezed his fingers on the back of her neck. "Sound good?"

She nodded.

Laura curled up on one side of the chair and took the Bible out of the box. She thumbed through it, read a verse here and there, but it didn't make sense. She was drawn to read. Compelled. But there just wasn't any way to know what it meant.

Jesse settled in beside her in the huge chair after setting her steaming mug of Folgers on the end table. This wasn't exactly how he had planned their first moments alone. Far from it. But whatever was going on with his little bride right this minute was more important than his urgency to get her under the covers of that big king bed in the back of the house. They would get there, eventually.

He stretched his arm along the back of the chair behind her head and threaded his long bony fingers through her hair. "Are you all right?"

"Yes, I'm fine. I just...," she glanced up at him, then looked back down. "I'm sorry, Jess. I seem to be ruining this night for us."

His hand grasped her shoulder and pulled her closer. "You've made me the happiest man alive, *Miz* Brandon. Nothing can ruin that for me. When something is bothering you, then it's bothering me too. Let's talk for a while and see if we can fix it."

Laura leaned her head back and sucked in a breath. "Mama told me all my life that people who believe that Jesus Christ was some kind of God were stupid and mentally retarded because there is no God. I never thought different until...until a few days ago." She sat up straight and patted the Bible lying in her lap. "Why do I believe this is real now? I mean...really sick people get well sometimes...Animals, too. Why, all of a sudden, do I seem to *know* that Jesus was some kind of Supreme Being?"

Before he could say a word, Laura covered her face with her hands and half laughed. "Oh geez. This is a horrible way to start our life together." Her hands fell to her lap. "Can we just start over. We're on our honeymoon, for Pete's sake. We can shelve this Jesus stuff for another time."

"No, we can't," Jesse said, his voice low and soft.

"What?" She glanced at him, surprised.

"This has been an issue for you, honey, all along. And I know the answer to why you believe that. It's the same exact reason why I, or anyone else…believes."

"Okay, I'm listening."

He couldn't help but smile at the eager *little girl* expression in her eyes. She was listening, all right. He took his arm from behind her and reached for the Book still in her lap. "This tells the answer…Judd showed me."

"What little I read in there…I don't see how anyone gets any answers from it…It reads like a foreign language."

Jesse flipped the pages, searching for the scriptures Judd had shown him. "In a sense, it is. This is God's Words. Guess you could say He lives in a foreign land. Here it is in the book of Matthew, chapter 16…Want me to read it to you?"

"Sure, I just hope I understand it."

"I think you will…I'll read it the way Judd read it to me.

Jesus came to His disciples saying, WHO DO MEN SAY THAT I AM?

And they said, Some say that you are John the Baptist,
Some say you are Elijah or Jeremiah, a great teacher
or a prophet.
    Then, Jesus said, BUT WHO DO YOU SAY THAT I
AM?
    And Peter, and Laura, answered and said, You are the
Christ,
    The Son of the Living God.
    And Jesus said to him, and to her,

Jesse leaned over and put his mouth against her ear and softly whispered the rest...

BLESSED ARE YOU, LAURA BRANDON: FOR FLESH AND BLOOD DID NOT REVEAL THAT TO YOU, BUT MY FATHER IN HEAVEN DID.

Laura went very still. She almost couldn't breathe. The sound of her name spoken that way, like it was truly written in there, personalized everything she had begun to believe.

Jesse watched her face and knew she got it.

"Oh...Jesse." She wrapped her arms around his broad chest and he laid the Bible on the floor beside the chair, then wrapped her up in his arms like a prized package. He held her tightly until she felt she would be consumed with the incredible love she was feeling. He seemed to know how comforting and full it made her to just be held this way. She thought this would be enough if neither of them ever moved away from this moment for the rest of their lives, until he lifted her face up to his and kissed her lips with a pure, raw passion. And when he raised his head, she watched him look at her with those glittering passion -drenched, come here gray slits. A lazy one-sided grin crooked his rugged face into that mischievous look she knew he must have greatly honored as a kid. Oh yeah. This cowboy of hers had a little rascal imp camped inside of a brain cell just lying in wait for an opportunity to show his stuff. She chuckled at the whole picture still gazing at her and in a flash, it was all over.

Both cups of coffee were left untouched and forgotten along with all of planet earth.

Jesse stood and easily lifted his bride in his arms. The joy in her eyes held his own like a magnet all the way down the hallway until he deposited her across the plaid quilted comforter on the bed, while he lay down beside her without relinquishing his hold. Before the sun rose a few hours later, clothes were draped around the room, in a chair, on the floor. Bed covers had been twisted on the bed, then piled on the floor and back on the bed again.

Three days later, Jesse and Laura relaxed in lounge chairs on the front porch of their lakeside hideout watching the first light of day break through on the eastern horizon. They would return to the ranch in the afternoon. Not once had they left the cabin in the past three days or hardly worn clothes, for that matter. They ate, drank, made love, bubble bathed, made love.

Many heart to heart talks over the past hours, in between the laughter and pranks and dares, culminated in the purest depth of unrestrained, wide-open-hearted meshing of two souls lives. The emotions that came from both of them within their most intimate moments took them into a depth of oneness that neither expected.

Laura discovered love in its truest form. She had discovered the love of a God. A God who, according to Jesse, had led her from the end of a life of one heartache after another, and into the arms and the love of a man whom she loved with all of her heart and soul.

She reached for her husband's hand. He had been off in thought since they sat down. "You okay?"

He grasped her hand and raised it to his mouth and kissed it. "I haven't been this *okay* in my entire life. It's just old selfish me hating that our time here is about to end. I've never known love in my life, Laura...until you." He looked down a few moments and swallowed hard. "I guess it scares me a little...To be this much in love with you. And, my God in Heaven...I have a son. What kind of God could love *me* enough to fill me this full of His best gifts on this earth. Boom, and I have it all."

He saw tears beginning to shimmer in her eyes. "Why are you crying?" He touched his finger to the drop that had spilled onto her cheek.

She could barely focus through the blur, but she saw Jesse's eyes welled full and she grinned. "I'm not crying...You are."

"Am not," he quipped dryly.

Suddenly, another little impish brain cell of the female persuasion gleamed at him from two squinty baby blue sparkles. "Anyway...you *beautiful* man...who says it's about to end. I happen to know of another cozy little Honeymoon Hideout a few miles up the road. A place called High Point Dude Ranch. It's available until next weekend."

"That right?" He looked at his watch. "Well, we've still got a few hours left right here. Just enough time for me to make you *THINK* ...*beautiful* man!"

She giggled, jumped up and ran inside, squealing with laughter all the way to the back of the lodge—Jesse hot on her heels.

****

PREVIEW OF

BOOK THREE IN THE

SURRENDERED SERIES

SURRENDERED III PREVIEW

Way before Kaitlyn had crossed the Wyoming state line, she and Bonnie had bonded fast and hard. A girl had never been crazier about a dog nor a dog about a girl. A one-stop shopping excursion to Wal-Mart before heading west out of Joplin, filled the front passenger bucket seat with Bonnie, atop her own fluffy, overstuffed pillow bed. The back floor carried a bucket of Kibbles and Bits and doggie treats, a leash and bottled water. Bonnie's new hot pink collar jingled with her tags from the vet's office and a not too pretty strip of plastic with Kaitlyn's name and cell number sharpied onto it just in case they got separated.

The pair spent their second night on the road in Jackson Hole at an old west style motel that welcomed canine guests. And until she had rolled into town and recognized some of the streets and shops, Kaitlyn hadn't once thought of Jesse Brandon. But with a heart-in-her-throat jolt, she remembered.

Her mind had felt so scrambled after losing her family and then Les.

After her father's death, her girlfriends, Lisa and Val had brainstormed a *fun* trip for the three of them to a dude ranch in cowboy-studded Wyoming. And Kaitlyn was ready to go off somewhere that she could forget it all for a few days. The three of them had laughed all the way from Missouri to Wyoming and run amuck in Jackson Hole at night after horseback riding, hiking, eating real chuck wagon grub, and flirting their wiggling backsides off with the cowboys at High Point Dude Ranch. The only problem, Kaitlyn fell for Jesse Brandon on the rebound from breaking up with Les Kane. And Jesse fell for her. She knew he was in love with her. She thought she loved him. One of those *love at first sight* things. A whirlwind romance right out of a typical romance novel.

Everything had happened so fast, including marriage plans, until her discovery just one week before she would have ruined not only her life, but Jesse's as well.

Her girlfriends had gone home to jobs and left her there in her pre-wedding bliss. Bliss that changed to stark reality after a home pregnancy test awakened her to the truth that she was still in love with Les Kane. He was the father of the baby she was carrying and she had to find out where he had gone.

All she remembered after that was her desperate desire to go home and to find Les. She knew she wasn't where she belonged.

That was all she remembered, until she pulled into Jackson Hole last evening. Lord help, it was a two-week whirlwind romance! Two weeks! Two weeks out of all the pain and regrets of her entire life. The memory of it kept her up most of the night, thoughts spinning with the horror of what she had done three years ago to a man who probably hated her after that with more passion than he had ever loved her with.

225

She had run away and left Jesse almost standing at the altar. One week before they would have exchanged wedding vows on the pavilion at High Point, Jesse's dude ranch, she asked some cowboy who was out painting fences to drive her to the closest airport, then paid him cash to forget he did it.

And until now, she had forgotten what she had done. She wondered what had happened in Jesse's life after the cruel, ruthless act she had committed against him.

Was it ever going to end, this list of conscience cleaners she'd written in rehab? She pulled her red leather journal out of her purse and added Jesse Brandon's name to that list. Her insides felt cold and sharp like splintered ice. Even remembering that God was always with her, would never forsake her, didn't warm her up this time. She just had to believe He was there, that He didn't lie to her, because she felt nothing, but achingly alone.

Around noon the next day, Kaitlyn checked out of the motel, with Bonnie in tow. The plan was to pay a visit to High Point and hopefully find Jesse quickly and offer her apologies. That thought sounded so hollow after what she'd done, but that's all she knew to do about it. And she *was* sorry for what she'd done to him. Shamefully remorseful. She decided if he hated her, it was her just due.

Thankfully, the motel offered Internet service. She was able to pull up a map showing directions to the Double OO where she hoped to find Les. The motel brochure rack had one for High Point. After comparing her directions for the day, she found both ranches on the same highway, a few miles apart.

That could be good, or not. She just really needed to get this day over with before she canceled it altogether. Then, by bedtime tonight, she and her four legged companion would be way down the road toward home.

Before pulling out from the motel, Kaitlyn closed her eyes a minute. *Father God, thank You for ordering my steps today.*

She hadn't been driving more than a few miles along a narrow, winding two-lane when her nerves got the best of her. How on earth did Les end up practically next door to that dude ranch? To Jesse Brandon's ranch? Oh, heaven help. She wasn't ready to face this. Les Kane was one event, but adding Jesse into the mix was overwhelming.

Kaitlyn's heart started pounding almost the instant raindrops began pelting her windshield. She thought maybe she should turn around.

Bonnie seemed to catch her master's panic attack. She sat up straight, ears alert and looked at Kaitlyn and whimpered.

And that's when it happened. She had smelled rain in the air all morning, but all at once a furious gust of wind and water attacked the driver's side of the car. Kaitlyn reached a hand out to comfort Bonnie as the steering wheel suddenly jerked to the right and out of her other hand. The sudden sheet of water cascading down the car windows blocked her view and the next thing she became aware of was the front passenger door hanging wide open and Bonnie disappearing out of it. The car had slowed almost gently and then thudded to a stop.

"Bonnie! Oh, no!" She couldn't see past the open car door with the typhoon-like wind and rain coming down, but she scooted across the seat and jumped out.

"Bon...nie. Come here, girl." She couldn't hear her own voice and knew Bonnie couldn't either. Luckily, she saw and felt the barbed wire fence just inches from the open car door and managed to mash the top down enough to high step over it."

"Bon...nie," she yelled again.

She began to run after a web of lightening lit the open field in front of her. Her feet seemed to be flying. She couldn't feel the ground, but a fearless adrenaline pushed her on. She had to find Bonnie.

It was amazing how fast the weather could change in this place. The poor little pup must be terrified. Kaitlyn kept running and calling to her. The rain poured and the wind wailed and whipped her heavy drenched hair across her face. She couldn't lose this dog. Bonnie was all she had. She must be scared to death. Maybe injured.

A dark cloud rolled in and joined the wind and rain, creating a new surge of panic. But the panic was for her lost Bonnie. She had never been able to save a single soul in her life.

Her mind whirled with old grief that seemed to blow in with each gust of the storm. Her mom had driven away without so much as a look back. Her brother died without one word of *I'll miss you.* And her dad had grieved to death over the loss of his son. She ran faster, frantic to outrun the taunting whistles in the wind. Les. Mae-Belle. Bonnie. And there was one more, but just as it came to throw the cruelest dart of all, the ground shifted under her feet, and then disappeared completely. She screamed and frantically clawed at the air. Then a body slamming thud shot pain from her right foot clear up to her head. Her whole body seemed to vibrate. Or maybe that was just the rain pounding her into the ground.

****